THE ROOTS OF THE GROUND

JAN FORTUNE

Published by Cinnamon Press
www.cinnamonpress.com
Office 49019, PO Box 92, Cardiff, CF11 1NB

The right of Jan Fortune to be identified as author of this work has been asserted by her in accordance with the Copyright, Designs and Patent Act, 1988. © 2020 Jan Fortune. ISBN 978-1-78864-119-7
British Library Cataloguing in Publication Data. A CIP record for this book can be obtained from the British Library.

All rights reserved. No part of this publication may be reproduced, stored in a retrieval system, or transmitted in any form or by any means, electronic, mechanical, photocopying, recording or otherwise without the prior written permission of the publishers. This book may not be lent, hired out, resold or otherwise disposed of by way of trade in any form of binding or cover other than that in which it is published, without the prior consent of the publishers.

Designed and typeset in Garamond by Cinnamon Press. Cover design by Adam Craig © Adam Craig.

Cinnamon Press is represented by Inpress and by the Books Council of Wales.

Acknowledgements

Thanks to the group of writers who accompanied me as I wrote this book, listening to first drafts of each chapter as they emerged. Thanks to Adam Craig for his careful reading and editing and for the cover. And thanks to Tamsyn Fortune-Wood for her enthusiasm and inspiration to complete a prequel to *The Standing Ground*. Thanks also to the village of Tanygrisiau, the setting for both books and my home for two decades.

THE ROOTS OF THE GROUND

To Merlin,
who is magical in Cymru and Bretagne

Prologue
Carmarthen County Hall, October 2028

Sian sits by the wall, holding her knees and rocking, eyes screwed closed. This is a mistake. She tells herself that Morfryn will hear about this and have her released. Soon. The place hasn't been a prison for almost a hundred years, the cells made into archive rooms decades ago. Yet here she is.

The door opens and she jumps to her feet. Two other women are thrust through the partly open entrance and the door slams behind them. They look as dazed as she feels and stand uneasily, not speaking until the older one breaks the silence.

'Who did you get on the wrong side of, then?'

Sian guesses the woman, tall and with a riot of unkempt blonde hair, must be in her early thirties.

'No one... I...'

'Must be someone. I've heard they're going for people who are expendable. Stories of them putting these things into kids in care. Regular prisoners of course. But now... They'll be putting them in everyone soon. Everyone in Wales, anyway. We're the testing ground.'

'Testing ground for what?'

'Implants, of course. What planet have you been living on?' It's the other woman who answers. She has dark curls and darker eyes. She's tiny but speaks with fierce intensity. Sian guesses she's about her age, late teens, early twenties.

'Implants?' Sian thinks she must sound stupid. She can't think properly. How can this be happening? 'No, they can't… I mean, I'll tell them I'm pregnant…'

The dark-haired young woman gives a bark of a laugh but the older one puts a hand on her arm.

'Pregnant? Whose? Is the dad…'

Sian sucks in air. 'He's a politician,' she says quietly.

'Oh, sweetheart…'

'But he… Morfryn wouldn't…'

'Morfryn Nazir Malik?"

Sian tries not to hear the contempt in the kind woman's voice.

The other laughs again. 'You like them old and powerful, eh?'

'You know he's just been made Minister for Connectivity?' the kind woman asks.

'For what? When?'

'Yesterday. How long have you been here?'

'Two days.'

Sian slumps back onto the ground by the wall and the blonde woman leans over her. 'He's the Devil, that one. I'm sorry, sweetheart. But listen. Maybe you'll be okay. Maybe it won't hurt the baby. They've been working on these implants for a couple of years now. Maybe…'

'Yeah, maybe your baby will be born with superpowers and save us all,' the dark-haired woman cuts in, sarcastically.

The door opens and two guards bar the exit.

'Sian Adhan Hughes?'

Sian stands up. 'That's me, but…'

'Save it for someone who cares,' the larger of the guards says.

'Come on, then. The Connectors haven't got all day,' the other adds. He moves forward and grabs her arm, jerking her ahead of him and out into the corridor.

Part 1

The Caverns

1

November, 2031

Gerhard Raven closed the virtual news site and rested his head in his hands. What now? He shook himself, stood and stretched.

'Well, my friend, at least I will try to save your son.'

He returned to the site and scanned the page beneath the headline:

FORMER MINISTER AND ENEMY OF E-GOV CUT DOWN IN PLANNED ATTACK

Regulators have confirmed that the terrorist who died in the failed insurgency of October 31 has now been identified as Morfryn Nazir Malik, former Minister of Connectivity, who absconded from his position two years ago to set up the radical terror group, Myrddin's Mutineers. The organisation is believed to operate from a forest location in Brittany, where it uses stolen technology to hide its whereabouts and activities. Before disappearing with sensitive state secrets, Malik, 44, rose to power as a Welsh politician of Arabic descent following a prestigious career as an IT entrepreneur whose work was critical in developing the architecture of E-Gov.

'It's hard to imagine why such a talented man whose worked paved the way for E-Gov, with all the benefits it has to offer us, should have betrayed his country and his calling,' commented

Tarquin Radley-Smythe, Malik's successor as Minister of Connectivity.

E-Gov has appealed to anyone who has information about the whereabouts of this dangerous and disturbed group to contact their local Regulators.

Meanwhile, E-Gov will be reaching out to the mother of Malik's child, Sian Adhan Hughes, to offer her support at this difficult time.

'Liars!' Gerhard shouted at the empty room.

He needed to reach Sian before the Carmarthen Regulators showed up at her door. No time to visit in person.

'Sian?'

'What? Who? I mean… how did you?…'

'Shh, you need to leave here. You need to follow me. Where's Emrys?'

'Asleep. I… Why should I…?'

'Sian, listen, you and Emrys are in danger. The Regulators are on their way. Morfryn was killed…'

'I know. He deserved it. He abandoned…'

'Please, listen. I'll explain… everything… but not here. You have to…'

'He's right, Mam. We have to leave now. Right now. It's Blaise, isn't it?'

Gerhard stared at the toddler in the living room doorway. 'Yes, I… Blaise is…'

'Your code name. He'll tell you everything when we're safe, Mam. Dad didn't abandon us, but the Regs will kill us.'

'Emrys?' Sian looked more shocked than Gerhard. 'When did you…?'

'Ask me later. You'll never get to find out if you don't follow Mr Raven now. Not that he's really here.' The child grinned and took his mother's hand. 'Now, Mam.'

Sian began grabbing items, but the boy shook her arm and pulled hard. 'Leave it.'

She scooped Emrys into her arms and ignored his protests about walking, following Gerhard, who marched ahead as Emrys continued to talk.

They scuttled along the main road, heads down and eventually turned into Reservoir Road, took the right hand fork as the road narrowed to an overgrown lane, and walked briskly until they reached the final house where the lane petered out into fields.

'We'll be safe here,' Gerhard told them, opening the door and directing them inside.

Sian deposited her son and slumped down onto the floor of the hallway, weeping.

Emrys patted his mother. 'Come and sit down, Mam.' He pulled gently and she stood up, sniffing and following her suddenly unfamiliar child into a large living room lined with book shelves.

'This place is…' she trailed away. 'I don't understand. I don't understand anything.' She began to cry more quietly.

'Let me fetch us something to drink and I'll do what I can to explain,' Gerhard told her.

'So you see, what your son told you on the walk here is true. Morfryn's position as Minister of Connectivity was his cover. He was one of those at the forefront of the technology that made E-Gov possible, but his invention was never meant for them. He was a wizard, of maths and logic, and of other things too. But like too many geniuses he didn't imagine how his work would be used for power. He didn't guard it closely enough and for a while he was naive, thinking E-Gov genuinely intended to make life better for people. When he realised the direction things were going he contacted a resistance movement in Brittany and together they set up Myrddin's Mutineers.

'He thought he'd have time to get you out, but they moved too fast. You were arrested before he realised how fast things were moving, thanks to a political rival who heard about your pregnancy. Someone angry at being passed over for what he felt was his rightful place in Cabinet. Of course, he had no idea about Morfryn's other powers and no idea how important your son would be. He was just an average power-hungry politician being vindictive. He probably hoped that using you as an early subject for the implants would cause a miscarriage or at least brain damage to your baby.'

'And who exactly is my son? Why's he so important? I mean…' Sian turned towards Emrys. 'I've never heard you talk before, well only… words…' She looked back at Gerhard. 'You know, like ordinary toddlers.'

Gerhard nodded. 'I'm sure Emrys didn't want to scare you, or put you at risk by letting you know too much. We need to remove your implant. The Regs will have already tracked you here in all likelihood, but by the time they arrive, we can make sure they can't see you.'

'But they won't believe you even if you can get these things out and hide us. They'll…'

'Trust him, Mam.'

'We're so sorry, for the intrusion, Dr Raven. We can't think how…'

'No problem at all, Regulator Reeves. We all have to be vigilant.'

'It just doesn't make sense, Sir. It…' The Regulator, a tall man in his late 30s, close cropped pale hair and paler skin, rubbed his forehead.

'These people are wily, I'm afraid. No doubt they… or their accomplices… have set up all kinds of decoys for just this occasion. I'm afraid my guess is that they'll already be overseas in a forest somewhere, plotting their next move. You mustn't blame yourself. They're dangerous people.'

Reeves nodded. 'I've heard that people used to think Malik was some kind of devil, even when he was in power. There was something not right about how he came up with all the tech in the first place. Not human, if you take my meaning?'

'Well, he wasn't powerful enough to outwit E-Gov in the end, thankfully, and I'm sure our rightness will win the day in the end.'

'Yes, Sir. Of course.' Reeves stood taller while behind him two shorter Regulators nodded their agreement. 'Well, thank you again for being so understanding, Dr Raven. And thank you for everything you do for E-Gov. We need artists like you.'

'How…?' Sian began to whisper, as the door closed behind the Regulators.

'Maths and magic, Mam,' Emrys said.

Gerhard smiled. 'The boy is right again. I'm afraid it's not something I can explain, but we can work a kind of illusion so they see only what we want them to. It's the same with the implants. To E-Gov we appear to be connected, but it's an illusion. Morfryn was one of the, shall we say, wizards? And I'm another. And of course, Emrys here, so no need to remove his implant. It's never operated. I'm sorry we had to cut yours out so hastily,' he added.

'So they couldn't see us, even me? It's not just the implants, it's…'

'You're right. Those of us who are… different. We're able to change how people perceive things. Maths and magic, as Emrys puts it.'

Sian shook her head. 'I'm so tired.'

'Of course you are. Let me show you your room. We have a long journey ahead, but sufficient to the day is its own trouble.'

Blaise

I have been known by many names. I have written the long-forgotten histories and myths, as Nennius, and have been the bard, Bleheris, and Blihis, writing and recounting the mysteries of the Grail. In each incarnation I have kept the chronicles of Brocéliande and of Cambria. Myrddin Emrys and of Artu, working in story and art. In this life, as Gerhard Raven, I write the tales and make installations of image and light to hold the memories. In this life, as in others, I will teach the young prophet, who will far outgrow me and who will love my daughter, Vivian. And she, in her turn, will be his own apprentice, outstripping him in ways of shapeshifting and sorcery, bringing him joy and grief, as her mother, my darling incarnation of Luned, will bring me.

This is how it will be, how it has always been, bringing the light of the Sun Child to this world again and again.

2

'Why Blaise as a code name?' Sian asked, as they drove north the next day.

'It's the name of Merlin's mentor in Robert Boron's thirteenth century account of the legends and in this lifetime too,' Gerhard answered.

Sian turned in her seat to look at her son, two and a half and fast becoming a mystery to her.

'Are you saying that Emrys is Merlin?'

Gerhard nodded. 'Myrddin Emrys. Yes.'

'Merlin's father was supposed to be a demon, wasn't he?'

'He was called that, yes. In some stories he's accused of being an incubus. In others he's called a black devil. Racism perhaps?'

Sian sucked in her breath. 'I'd never thought of that. But this is… I mean, those are stories. It's the 2030s, not the Middle Ages or Roman Britain or some Celtic forest in Brittany. This is real, it's…' She sighed. 'I've no idea what this is.'

'It's complicated but think about it like this— E-Gov can put a chip in your body and you can visit any site it permits you to see. You can smell the flowers that you see on a website meadow. In the Middle Ages that would have been wizardry beyond imagining. We simply have another sort of wizardry, though it's not the same for all of us. We have various skills. Not all of us use shapeshifting or illusion.'

'It's still hard to take in.' Sian was silent for a while. 'Are we going to a group of others like you and Emrys?'

'No,' Gerhard glanced from the road to Sian's worried face. 'They're regular people, but with a knack for resistance. We're going to The Standing Ground, Y Tir.'

'So there really is a resistance movement in North Wales? How come they haven't been wiped out?'

'They're well hidden. A bit of magic in that, though they don't realise it. And they've taken to the old mines. There are caverns underground bigger than cathedrals. Plenty of room for a small community to disappear into. E-Gov started destroying towns and villages along the border in the North back in '23, one of its first policies when there were early signs of resistance.

'They thought they'd starve out the places further in, but the North Welsh formed good relationships with the newly-united Ireland and with Brittany. E-Gov moved in to do a mass evacuation and resettlement last Spring. They didn't find The Standing Ground members, only abandoned houses but they cleared the towns and villages to the east and all the way to the border.'

'None of that's been in any news.'

'Of course. E-Gov doesn't want to advertise that it's forcibly relocating people to break up communities who might not agree to its new normal. But they had a cover story prepared in case of leaks— they would claim they had to evacuate the people in the border towns because of their high infection rates. It was part of Deep Cleaning for Britain, though they never needed the story in the end. Managed to keep it quiet.'

Sian leant forward. 'So what really happened?'

'Some people were moved to awful suburbs of the Midlands overspill, or to towns further from the borders and around Birmingham or Manchester. Some people died and those in Y Tir disappeared into the mines. Not many. And it's a hard existence, but they persist. There's a spattering of others in a couple of forest communities and around the Llanberis quarries and two others on Anglesey, but that's it for the free folk of this island.'

'And none of them have tags?'

'Not one.'

'And they'll let us join them?'

'They will. It's early days and they've got a lot of thinking to do to rid themselves of old ideas of how to organise. There are some good people there. Tomas Selwyn and his wife, Megan. They have a son about a year older than Emrys. And Gwynne and Anwen Hughes, who have a little girl, though sadly Gwynne will have died before you can meet him.'

'Was he sick?'

No, an accident. His horse slipped on a bank and he suffered a head injury as he fell into the water so drowned... he was... sometimes those of us who might be called wizards lead… I suppose you might say, double lives. He…'

'… was my dad.' Emrys said quietly from the back seat.

'What?' Sian swivelled from Gerhard to Emrys and back again. 'This just goes on making less and less sense.'

'Morfryn Malik and Gwynne Hughes were one person.'

'Did he… did he have children with, with this other Hughes woman?'

'Anwen,' Emrys answered for Gerhard. 'Yes. I have a sister. Gwenddydd.'

'I'm sorry it's so much to take in at once,' Gerhard added. 'But the main thing is, you're safe.'

'Perhaps. You said there are some good people, but you also said they have to rid themselves of old ways. What does that mean?'

'They're afraid and they're clinging to an old hierarchy at the moment. And there's some religious puritanism that makes them…'

'Less welcoming?'

'You could say that.'

'So they might not take us in?'

'They will take you in. But it might not always be easy. Their current leader is not an happy man. Ifor Tigaen, he's called. He's easily disturbed by anything that appears 'different' so…'

'So a mixed race eloquent two-year-old won't be exactly to his liking.' It was Sian who finished for Gerhard this time.

'You will need to be cautious,' Gerhard agreed.

'Will you be staying with us?'

Gerhard shook his head. 'I'll be going to Brittany. I only stayed in Carmarthen to be at hand for you and Emrys. You were always under surveillance but we hoped to get you out to join Morfyn at some point. I'll need to take his place now… now that he's no longer with us.'

'But…'

'I'll always watch out for you and Emrys and I feel his path and mine will become one again in the future. But until then…'

'I can't persuade you? Even for a while, I mean till they accept us or…'

'You'll be fine. And I have a family to return to. My wife is expecting our first child.'

'Oh, oh that's… then of course you must go.'

Myrddin Emrys

I found my mentor the day my father's death was announced by E-Gov. In another life, Blaise had protected Merlin and his mother. He had mentored Merlin as he learnt to shapeshift and see past and future, and had chronicled Merlin's life. In this life, Gerhard Raven, known as Blaise to his comrades in Myrddin's Mutineers, would teach me illusion and art and introduce me to the love of my life. But that was still a long way off.

Sitting in the car, listening to my mother, anxious about our future, I drifted into the stories of another time, stories of Vortigern, the Ifor Tigaen of his time.

Sixteen hundred years ago, a king, fleeing the invading Saxons, settled on a mountain in Eryri to build his fortress. From there he could see for miles. The ground was firm and the rivers ran clear. And so the building began.

Each day the masons worked. Each night the walls fell. And so it continued, whatever was built by day, fell at night. No threats could make the masons construct anything that could stand. And so Vortigern assembled every wise man, seer and magician in Eryri and, after consulting, they told him the land was cursed and the only thing that would make it settle was the blood of an innocent child. Not any child, but one whose mother was human and whose father was of the otherworld.

But how to find such a child? They searched the area but there was no such child. Instead, they sacrificed children whose fathers were unknown. Still the tower fell each night. So the search was widened and at last a child from Caer Myrddin was discovered. His mother was Adhan and his father was unknown, though there were rumours that he was a demon.

The boy was prepared for sacrifice but before he could be killed he called out to Votigern, telling him he was a fool, that his death, like the deaths of the fatherless children before him, would make no difference because under the mound where the fortress was being built, was an underground lake. And in the lake were two warring spirits, one white dragon and one red, who fought each night, pulling the fortress apart.

Convinced, Vortigern ordered the mound to be excavated and there, as predicted was the lake, hot water bubbling in it. But Emrys, also known as Myrddin, walked into the water and summoned the dragons, who woke and began to fight. At last, the red dragon prevailed and the white dragon fled. The red dragon returned to live quietly beneath the lake and Vortigern's fortress, Dinas Emrys, was built.

And now we will meet again.

3

When Gerhard had finished introducing Sian and Emrys, there was silence. Ifor Tigaen gazed at them, unmoving. Finally he stood, towering over the table around which a small group had gathered to meet them.

'We're not a refugee camp for the cast-offs of disgraced politicians,' Ifor said at last.

Emrys scanned the faces around the table. A tiny woman in her fifties with red-gold hair sat next to a man who looked remarkably like her, no doubt her son. Liam, Gerhard had said as he had gone around the table making introductions. On the other side of the woman, Angharad, was her daughter, Betsan, seated next to her husband, Sion Roberts, a dark-haired, stocky man in his early thirties, with eyes almost the colour of coal. The woman who had just lost her husband, Anwen, kept her eyes down but he could see how red-rimmed they were. She fingered a ring on her right hand, a knotted red-gold band set with a red stone that Emrys felt he should recognise. Tomas shook his head slowly as Ifor spoke and sucked in his breath slightly, but it was Angharad who stood to face him, fixing him with bright blue eyes so that he blinked and stepped back slightly. The little boy of about five, who sat on the floor playing with a wooden toy horse, stopped and looked up at his grandmother.

'If Gerhard says Morfryn Malik was fighting E-Gov, then they're kith and kin. In any case, we're not exactly over-run with people queuing up to join us. And Sian's a Hughes like Gwynne, God rest him.'

Emrys saw Anwen nod and look up. She smiled at him and his mother and Sian smiled back at the woman who'd apparently loved the same man in a different guise.

'If you think we've got the resources to feed more weak women and scrawny kids, then…'

Sian pulled Emrys tighter on her lap. 'My son's not scrawny and I'm not weak,' she said, her voice quiet but fierce.

'Well, we'll soon find out. Living in these caves sorts out the weaklings pretty efficiently.'

It was Anwen's turn to flare into action, pulling Ifor down to her eye level by his arm. 'Don't you dare suggest Gwynne died because he was weak.' She took a deep breath and pulled herself up, still holding onto his arm, her face close to his. 'You'd have starved long back without the work of Gwynne and others like him. Or died of the virus that took good people like Alun Parry when they could have put their own safety first, but instead went on caring for weaklings like you.'

She sat down heavily and breathed hard.

'I didn't mean…' Ifor glanced towards the tiny woman who had spoken first, still standing, watching him with bright eyes and a quizzical look. 'No offence to Alun, Angharad. He was an amazing doctor, a hero, we all know that. And Gwynne…' He turned back to face Anwen, who was visibly restraining tears. 'Gwynne's a great loss to all of us, of course he is. Without his farming… We're all grateful. It's just that I care about this community so much, you see, so much it worries me that we might be threatened by… well, by… people we don't know whether we can count on.'

'That's most laudable,' Tomas spoke at last and Emrys noticed how the whole room exhaled in relief. Angharad Parry visibly relaxed and her grandson, Gethin, resumed his play. Even Ifor Tigaen looked relieved and sat down. 'We know you've got the community's interests at heart, Ifor. We're grateful for that. Caution's a fine thing, but so is trust and we've always trusted Gerhard. And a community that shows no kindness isn't long for this world. We know you'll take the whole picture into account.'

'Quite.' Emrys watched Ifor puff out his chest slightly as he spoke 'That's exactly the direction I was heading in,' Ifor added. 'We have to ask the right questions, not be rash, but we also have to show generosity and Gerhard has never given anything but good advice. So, I'd like you all to join me in welcoming Sian and little Emrys to Y Tir.

There were nods and murmurs. 'Well-played,' Emrys heard Gerhard whisper to Tomas. 'Take care of them for me.'

Tomas nodded and Emrys grinned at him.

Out loud Gerhard said, 'I have to get back on the road. I've got a long journey.'

It was Tomas who showed Sian and Emrys around the labyrinthian community. He was less laconic than he had been at the meeting and his voice warmed to telling them the history of the place.

'Two-hundred and fifty chambers in twenty-five miles of tunnel,' he began, 'though not all of them can be inhabited. There are sixteen levels going down nearly two thousand feet. Viciously cold down there but even the mid-levels are too cold to be liveable and anyway, they're dangerous, liable to flooding. But the caverns in the first six-hundred feet give us a lot of space to play with.'

'This isn't too bad,' Sian commented as they entered an enormous cavern at five-hundred feet depth.

Tomas nodded. 'They'd be about five to seven degrees left to their own devices. This cavern and the next were used for storing and maturing cheeses, fitted with electricity about four years before the first pandemic and the flues meant we could put in four big wood stoves with chimneys so could raise the temperature and not cause health problems from the smoke.'

Water dripped incessantly down the gigantic cavern walls, and Emrys gazed upwards at ferns growing in clusters on their great height. Sian hefted him into a different position on her hip.

'Walk now,' he said in toddler-speak.

She looked down at the cavern floor, uneven with shards of leftover slate in every size.

'Walk now,' he repeated.

She set him down but grasped his hand. 'Stay close. It's slippy.'

There were wooden partitions around the cavern, dividing it into makeshift family spaces. Wooden walls and a variety of roofs, some like sheds, some with waterproofed fabric stretched across and nailed tight so that the whole place murmured and buzzed like a vast hive.

In the third cavern, bigger than the previous two together, the lighting glowed purple and amber and there were remnants of plastic tubes and what looked like monstrous spider webs hanging above them. Tomas followed their gaze.

'There was a kind of adventure centre in here in the twenties,' he told them. 'People used to come for miles, from all over the world, to bounce on trampolines inside huge nets. I never saw the appeal but it was very popular. There's a couple of empty shacks near mine and Megan's just along here if you fancy one of those.'

'Thank you. We'd like that,' Sian said.

'We've got a boy a bit older than Emrys. Geraint. He's three-and-a-half. But his mam's not too clever at the minute.'

'Is it anything serious?'

Tomas wiped a hand across his forehead and sighed. 'She's one of those that owes her life to Alun Parry, Angharad's husband. Her and Ifor and a lot more beside.' He paused. 'We didn't have much virus here at first, got off light compared to a lot of areas. But there was more and more pressure for tourism to start up again. Suddenly it was ripping through the villages like wildfire and there weren't enough beds in the hospitals. Some ended up in a makeshift place over at Bangor university. Like a war zone. And there was an old psychiatric unit over at Penrhyn, already near derelict, where beds were set up in these grim Victorian corridors. Not enough ventilators, not enough protective gear for the doctors and nurses.' He stopped again.

'I'm sorry… if you'd rather not…' Sian began.

He shook his head. 'Best you know a bit about us. We both got it and it's an odd one, usually it took men harder. None of us expected Ifor to make it. But with us it was Megan that got the worst. She wanted to stay at home but her breathing was so bad… I didn't think I'd see her again when the ambulance came for her, the paramedics in masks they'd had to buy for themselves, not proper medical ones either.' Tomas leant a hand against the damp cavern wall as though for support. 'But Alun and his team… Anyway, it was Alun that didn't make it. I thank him every day to still have my Megan, but her lungs were damaged and she's… it's hard to pinpoint but she's never been quite the same…

I was terrified all through the pregnancy, but Anwen was there for the birth, and Angharad too.'

'Anwen's a midwife?'

'Doctor. Her husband was our main farmer, so quite a pair. Very sudden that. Terrible loss.'

Sian nodded.

'Forgive me,' Tomas said. 'You've just lost Emrys's dad and I'm telling you sad tales.'

Sian smiled. 'I hadn't seen Morfryn since I was first pregnant. But I did miss him. And now…' She straightened and smiled. 'But I've got Emrys and I've found The Standing Ground,' she said briskly.

'Yes, and don't let that fox, Ifor, colour your ideas of us.'

'Is it just him?'

Tomas appraised Sian carefully, a hand to his mouth. 'I wish I could say yes, but there's been a lot of unease recently. We've been struggling for supplies, had losses, things go missing.'

'How do you feed everyone?'

'A few farmers, people like Gwynne, have made all the difference. It's dangerous work. You can't farm underground except for mushrooms. The places are camouflaged to look derelict as much as possible but to be honest I'm constantly amazed there haven't been air strikes on them.'

Emrys squeezed his mam's hand. 'Maths and magic,' he whispered.

'But for the most part we get supplies from Ireland. That's courtesy of your friend Gerhard and the Mutineers. He's a pretty extraordinary character. Apparently, a brilliant artist too, though I've never seen any of the work, and a tech genius as well. He trades with Ireland—they get high tech and we get fed.'

'But some of it's going astray?'

'Recently yes. And not just food. Blankets, fabric, prefabricated metalwork that we use for shoring up areas liable to slips, IT hardware, herbs and medicines.'

'That's a lot to lose.'

Tomas nodded. 'Yes, and sadly it starts rumours and factions. But enough bad news. You need to get settled in. Just along here…'

Luned

I come from myth, from time before memory. I am not who I seem to be and yet I am who I seem to be. I am Luned, mistress of the moon, who serves the lady of the lake. I am Creirwy, daughter of Ceridwen of the White Song, goddess of poetry who dwells under Lake Bala. I am present and I am invisible, guiding the lost through the otherworld, Annwn. I am the priestess who carries the vessel to bring healing and light. I send my spirit out to dwell in those who cocoon me deep in their dreams and to those who carry me to light the path of every step.

4

By New Year, Sian had started to relax into their new life. But in February the disasters began.

Sian heard about Megan's death from Anwen, who stood in their doorway looking grey and defeated.

'I can't believe we've lost her.' Anwen's voice was flat with exhaustion.

Sian ushered her in and made her sit down. 'I'll go and make tea. Wait here.'

When she returned, Emrys was in Anwen's lap, rocking her as she sobbed softly. Anwen glanced up. 'I'm so sorry. I…'

'No, don't be.'

Emrys stroked Anwen's face.

'Children can be so wise,' Sian said nervously, setting the tea on a stool where Anwen could reach it.

'Yes, especially when they're special children like Myrddin Emrys Malik.'

Sian froze.

'Sorry, I'm to tired of pretending,' Anwen went on. 'I think we shared a very special man who shapeshifted through our lives. I think Emrys and Gwen are half-brother and sister. Do you agree?'

'Yes. I suppose Gwynne, Morfryn as I knew him, was why E-Gov couldn't see your farms?'

Anwen nodded.

'How many people know… I mean…'

'Hardly anyone. I think Tomas has his suspicions.' She began to cry again. 'Sorry. You'd think a doctor would be inured but... I keep thinking of him raising Geraint alone.'

'Like both of us.'

'Yes.'

'What was it?'

'Pneumonia. She had such weakened lungs after the virus. She's not the only one. Liam Parry is seriously ill too.'

'Tomas told me about the virus, about coming through and everything Alun Parry did.'

'Amazing man. He trained us. Me and three others. Angharad taught us too, all the herbal lore she knows. There's too much loss.'

'Yes.'

They sat in silence for a while until Anwen said. 'Thank you. I know it could have been strange, awkward between us, but I feel like I know you, have known you for longer than a couple of months. I'd better go and fetch Gwen and Geraint. Betsan's looking after both of the them at the moment and I'm going to keep Geraint with me a day or so, though Tomas wants to tell him straight away.'

A week after Megan's funeral, Liam Parry died of pneumonia, leaving his young wife, Nerys to raise their son, Gethin. Another child with only one parent.

The cave-in came in March. It was a Sunday afternoon when Emrys, not even three-years-old, ran past the open doors of the shacks shouting, 'Tell them to run, tell them to run.'

He ran towards Cavern Three, the soft white noise of ever-present drips crescendoing to a gushing sound before cracks like thunder reverberated below. Knots of people appeared in doorways as the child ran past, into the cavern from where the surging hiss emanated. Another boom of thunder and people came running from Cavern Three, some sodden, others speckled in needles of slate, one of them carrying Emrys in his arms.

Three families were lost from the farthest end of the drowned cavern, others injured. Anwen and her fellow doctors worked long hours but still there were more, including Ifor's mother, Catrin, and Nerys Parry.

Now, Gethin had neither parent, only his nain, Angharad Parry, and his aunt and uncle, Betsan and Sion. The whole community fell into hushed mourning.

And then, after a subdued Easter, the virus struck.

'We can't take any more,' Ifor pronounced, at a meeting in one of the large uninhabited spaces just below Caverns One and Two, a space big enough to crowd in hundreds of shivering and demoralised people, standing in tiny knots, keeping their distance from other families.

The murmurs of assent rippled through the assembly.

'Life in the caverns has always been hard. It's the price of our freedom. But in the last months our suffering has grown and grown. Our supplies are going missing, we've lost good people like Megan Selwyn, Liam and Nerys Parry, my own dear mother, Catrin. We've suffered the first cave-in since we moved here. And now we're prey to this infection that we thought we'd seen the last of nearly four years ago.' He paused to scan the faces of those he could make eye contact with. 'Infections don't spring from nowhere. There has to be a carrier. A spreader. We know that from the years of pandemics we've survived.'

Murmurs rose and Ifor let the uneasiness spread before gesturing for quiet. 'I know there are doubters amongst us, nay-sayers who think humans call the shots in this world. But we have always been a godly people. A clean-living people.' In his next pause there was not a sound, hundreds of people holding their breath. 'But now we have allowed outsiders to join us. And, I have to ask you today, is this kindness or an act of self-destruction?'

There was a smattering of shouts, some in protest, but he raised his voice to go on. 'And we know that one among us is not of our people. Malik. Where is that name from? Was he even a man? Was he a demon? And even if he was human, he came from who knows where? I know…' he raised his voice louder as murmurs of anger rose against him. 'I know it's not the done thing to talk about race, but that black demon's child is here, in our community, and we're dying. A strange child who can sense a cave-in before it even happens, but warns us too late. A dark child, carrying who knows what? Now, I know we took them in because we're a trusting, open-hearted people. And I'm not saying that all the deaths can be put down to… though God knows, the devil has his ways… But this virus. How did it get here? From where? From who?'

He let the uproar, for and against, rage around the cavern. From the height of the wooden platform he stood on, he smiled towards Sian, a thin smile of triumph. She held Emrys tightly to her, inching through the gaps in the knots of families, towards the edge of the cave.

'And the mistress of the devil… what part has she played?'

'Enough!' Tomas was on the platform commanding calm. 'Enough! This is not the Middle Ages. We are not…'

'The Bible tells us not to suffer a witch to live…'

'Enough!' Tomas's voice was like a whip bringing order. 'If you have to quote the Bible, get it right.' He faced Ifor, standing close so that Ifor backed off and pulled up the fabric face mask he had round his neck. 'The Bible says nothing about witches, but it does say do not suffer a poisoner to live amongst you. And what I'm hearing from you is surely the most toxic poison.'

There were murmurs, assent and dissent.

Sian tried to control her shaking, glancing around. The exit to the cavern was on the other side of the assembly. Figures in masks, hoods pulled up, moved towards her from three sides, the damp wall with its perpetual song of drips behind her. She clutched Emrys so tight he pushed back against her.

'Shh, Mam, Shh, it's okay, Tomas'll…'

She noticed Anwen edging towards her, caught the glint of the ruby in Anwen's ring as she put an arm around her as the men moved closer, closer, so close… Sian screamed and…

Myrddin Emrys

Druids learn slowly and by heart. We learn that the human spirit is strong, stronger still when it follows the seasons and the pulse of all life. Always there are tyrants, they rise and fall, wielding the same weapons over and over, weapons that betray their emptiness of heart and soul: fear, repression, lies, even death. But when our souls are not destroyed, when we refuse to surrender hope, their power wanes. Druids persist because we know that the human spirit is indomitable.

Where do I come from? From myth and history, from mist and reality. From maths and magic. From Carmarthen: the child without a father or the child whose father was called the Devil. From the wild woods, a prophet drunk on grief from all the violence I have witnessed. I am all of this and none of it.

I am a seer to kings: to the fools like Vortigern and to those, like Aurelius Ambrosius, who held back the darkness for a time, and to Artu, who returns, as I do, again and again, a light in the darkness.

5

Sian woke in Anwen's shack. Emrys and Gwen were playing, building an impossibly high tower of wooden blocks.

'Dragons woke up…' Emrys roared and clashed two small carved dragons into the base of the tower, Gwen rolling in laughter as it toppled.

'Again, again…' she commanded between giggles.

'Sian, you're awake.' Anwen bent over her.

'I… How did I get here?'

'I'm not actually sure. You screamed and Tomas shouted at Ifor's heavies to not dare touch you and then… you'd gone. I mean… vanished.'

'I don't understand, I…' Sian looked at Emrys playing with Gwen and Anwen followed her gaze.

'He's… he's not like other toddlers, is he?' Anwen whispered. 'I don't mean… I mean… He's telling Gwen the story of Vortigern and Merlin, isn't he?' And he's not even three.'

Sian flushed. 'He's… I…' She began to sob.

'Oh, Sian, no, I'm so sorry. I didn't mean anything bad by it. It's not easy for us, is it? Morfryn Malik didn't look like my Gwynne, but they were one and the same. And Gwynne, well, he always… he was different too. I always knew he was more than he seemed… and… well, he had something special in him that kept our farms invisible from E-Gov drones. I'm not without my own secrets, I suppose. We understood it didn't need talking about.'

'A bit of maths and magic.'

Both women turned towards Emrys.

He grinned. 'Sometimes life's better as a mystery to live…'

'Not a puzzle to be solved,' Anwen finished for him. 'An almost three-year-old quoting Kierkegaard.' She turned back to Sian. 'You know you can trust us. Me and Tomas Selwyn, Angharad Parry and her daughter Betsan and Betsan's husband, Sion. And others too. Ifor has his followers, gullible idiots or those wound up with religious fanaticism, but there are more good people.'

'How did he become the leader?'

'Ha! Rich family, used to lording it over others. That and no one with sense wanted power, so he stepped in out of the goodness of his heart. Plus, there's always been an unspoken understanding that he was easier to keep an eye on while he was playing god as long as it didn't really effect anything. Ifor holds meetings while other people get on with farming or making trade deals or building shacks… He was out of harm's way playing politics… at least till now.'

There was a knock and Tomas's voice on the other side of the door. Anwen opened it and he ducked in quickly.

'They're fine,' Anwen told him. 'And I'm just about to make tea. Come in.'

'Only if...' He hovered by the door.

'You won't infect us, Tomas. Ifor's wrong about the virus. Nasty as it is, it's not like the previous ones we've seen. Mam and me think it's more like a norovirus, but milder and with a few other differences, like hitting us in summer and having a really rapid infection and illness period. It's definitely infectious but you're not going to breathe it onto us or us onto you and it's not as dangerous, as long as people keep hydrated, especially the old or children.'

Tomas came into the room and sat on a large floor cushion covered in a sheep fleece. 'Well, I don't suppose it's exactly good news about this bug, but it's better than we're being led to think. Thank you.' He glanced at the children. 'Gwen, can I borrow Emrys a moment?'

Gwen nodded solemnly. 'Dragons,' she said, giving the tower a last swipe and giggling.

'Dragons indeed,' Tomas agreed. 'Is that your diagnosis, Myrddin Emrys?"

Emrys stood in front of Tomas and nodded. 'Yes. The community can't be safe while it's divided. Even the rocks of the cavern know it.'

'Ifor's the white dragon?'

Emrys nodded again. 'Ifor Tigean is bleeding the community for his own profit. All the missing supplies are because of him. He's been re-trading a portion of whatever arrives from Ireland. He's dealing with a border community in the Subs and another in South Wales. Once he has enough money he'll leave and betray The Standing Ground's whereabouts to E-Gov. He thinks he'll get a political position in return for telling them our location. They'll probably just kill him, of course.'

'And you are the red dragon? The community can't survive two dragons at once, eh?'

'That's right. It can't.'

'So where do I find proof about Ifor?'

Emrys considered. 'It's in me. And I can show you the trail if you bring me a computer. Later, you can show it to others. But we need to confront Ifor with the evidence. That would be better without an audience. He's already trying to convince people I'm a demon's child. If they hear me prophesying Ifor's future, plenty more will believe him.'

'I'll see to the computer and arrange a meeting with Tigean. But first some tea and food. It's been a long day.'

Emrys smiled at his mother and Anwen, who were following the conversation. 'That's a beautiful ring, Mrs Hughes,' he said. 'I think I heard of one just like it in a story.'

Anwen coloured and smiled. 'Did you now? A story of dragons?'

He grinned. 'A story of Eluned the Fortunate. It was in Tri Thlws ar Ddeg Ynys Prydain, I think.'

She nodded. The Thirteen Treasures of the Island of Britain, eh?'

'Yes. And the ring of Eluned is the most powerful artefact of all. Doesn't it grant invisibility when the stone is concealed?'

'I think that's the story, yes.' She grinned at him. 'Now, I'm going to help Tomas make us some food.'

Luned

The ring of Eluned the Fortunate is the most powerful of all the magic artefacts of the Isles of Britain. When did it come to me? I remember it only after we buried Gwynne and yet it feels like I have known it forever. Perhaps it is that it has always known me.

Always, I guide and protect those who serve the light, who help it to be reborn. We live in such dark times, have lived so long in dark times.

I was a teenager when the first pandemic came, more bored than afraid as lockdown dragged on and in Wales was longer and harsher than in England. The second wave came fast and then the yearly bouts of wearing facemasks and keeping our distance, the restrictions on travel and school online for months of each year and only ever part-time during the other terms.

We grew accustomed to tyrants acting for us in the name of our best interests. Once we'd been wrenched out of Europe, trade collapsed and the country, impoverished and full of fear, was an easy picking for the despots. E-Gov was introduced one 'obvious' increment at a time. Dissent was unpatriotic.

But in a corner of North Wales, the years of sickness and isolation showed us that we must become more community-sufficient. And across the world, the virus and it's terrible mutations forced even the vilest of governments to face the need to ban coal-fired power stations, decrease their reliance on burning through the earth.

Y Tir is a fragile place, full of courage and hope. And I will use what power I have to hold a space for the light, not knowing what might come.

6

'You're telling me the cavern collapsed because there are two dragons in residence, you and me, and they—or we—will go on sending shock waves through the earth until one is vanquished and leaves?'

Ifor grimaced and looked towards Tomas, who had sat quietly while young Emrys told his contemporary version of the the Tower of Vortigen at Dinas Emrys, just six miles as the crow flies from their cavern at Llechwedd, even closer to those of their community living in the one habitable cavern beneath Cwmorthin.

'He's the devil's child, alright, Tomas.'

'I think not,' Tomas replied. 'He may be speaking in metaphors but the evidence he's shown me of your creaming off essential supplies to sell to the Subs—there's nothing story book about that, Ifor.'

'You're making it up.'

'I've copied the evidence to several platforms and the key to your accounts is already safely in the hands of Constantine's Daughters and Sons,' Emrys said.

'Who?'

'The tech guys amongst Myrddin's Mutineers in Brittany. They can make it public in seconds. Either way, you'd better run. Either your Saxon so-called allies in E-Gov will kill you or the Daughters and Sons will hunt you down.'

The day Ifor Tigean vanished from Llechwedd, several delegations arrived at Tomas's door to ask him to take over leadership of the community. He shook his head each time, told them it was too soon for him to think of such a thing, only three months after losing Megan, but they kept returning, all through the day, ones and twos, small and larger groups.

'I'm no politician,' Tomas said, over and over.

'That's why we need you, Tomas,' countered Sion Roberts. Behind him others nodded. 'We need people who aren't interested in power. And you're the one who found those sites with all the dodgy stuff Ifor had been up to. We need a leader who's clever, who won't let anyone fool us again.'

Tomas sucked breath between his teeth. 'Power corrupts, Sion. No one's immune from that.'

'We have to have a leader, Tomas. We…'

'Do we?'

'Pardon?' Sion ran a hand through his thick sandy-brown hair. 'I don't think I follow you.'

'At least let's share it, eh? A group, like Ifor's so-called advisory committee but with actual power, by consensus. Different ages, people from different caverns. Not too big mind, nothing unwieldy. And strictly limited powers. Enough to see us safe, keep us trading and fed. No more.'

'You'll be part of it?'

Tomas nodded. 'For a while, anyway.'

'Chair it?'

The group behind Sion chimed in with their support.

'Let's see if people agree first, shall we?'

'Deal.' Sion breathed a gust of relief and grinned, but almost instantly resumed looking serious and tired. 'Do you think he'll give our location away? Run to E-Gov?'

An uneasy murmur went through the knot of women and men standing around Tomas's door. He nodded. 'I'm sure he will.'

'How long do we have?'

'Who knows. He's got a long walk ahead of him and he's not the fittest of men. He might do it in two days, maybe three if we're lucky.'

There were audible groans from the group.

'We should meet quickly, Tomas, tonight. We can get a group together. How many?'

Tomas shook his head. 'I've got no expertise in this, Sion, but I'd say no more than twelve.'

'We're on it. 7 o'clock in the meeting room?'

Tomas nodded wearily. 'I'll be there.'

'We've got several problems,' Tomas began, scanning the group of anxious faces. 'Morale is bad after winter. I'm not the only person to have lost someone I loved. Geraint isn't the only child with a mother or father missing. And there are people with injuries after the fall and we've got overcrowding in the shacks until we can build more to replace those flooded or crushed. And now we find the person who should have been looking after our interests was selling essential supplies. We're low on food and a lot of fuel was stored in Cavern Three. All that wood's washed away. But none of that's as urgent as what might be coming. We may only have a few days before E-Gov is down on us. We're not a rumour anymore. We're the enemy.'

'We don't have a chance, do we?' It was Sion who spoke what they were all thinking.

'I can't let myself think that,' Angharad said quietly. 'Even now, with not a clue what to do, I can't countenance just sitting here and waiting for them to…'

'What do you think they'll do, Tomas?' Anwen asked.

Tomas shook his head. 'Maybe they'll round us up and take us to those places where they break people's spirit, put their chips in us and scatter us to lives of desperation. Or maybe…' He took a deep breath. 'I know we feel hidden in here and there's a chance we can defend tunnels. We know the caverns. They don't. But, on the other hand, they could flood us, even reign fire down on us… I… I think we might be better back in the villages, out of the mines.'

Twenty conversations erupted between twelve people. Tomas put his head in his hands, then rallied, but before he could speak again, Sian rushed into the room.

'Tomas! Tomas!'

They all stood and Anwen put a hand on Sian's arm.

'It's Emrys. I can't find him. I can't…' She began to sob, leaning heavily on Anwen, who eased her onto a chair and knelt beside her.

'She'll sleep now,' Anwen told Tomas a few hours later. 'Still no sign?'

Tomas shook his head and wiped a hand across his eyes. He felt so much older than thirty-three. The meeting had crumbled in chaos and fear while search parties were set up. He'd told Anwen to hold off using sedatives for a while. Surely the boy couldn't have gone far. He was clever, not like a toddler at all. But when team after team came back, pale, exhausted and shaking their heads, he'd told her to do whatever she thought best.

'I think he's safe,' Anwen told him.

He wanted to believe her but the thought of flooded caverns and caves with hundred foot sheer drops round blind corners… They'd been lucky not to lose a child to the terrain already. But Emrys… the boy who had told him about Ifor barely a week ago. The boy who was playing out the story of Vortigern in the twenty-first century. The little red dragon. Could he really have simply wandered to his death?

'Tomas?'

He shook himself. 'Sorry. I'm bone-tired and can hardly think. I'm glad Sian's sleeping. And I hope you're right.'

'I think you are right about the villages too. We shouldn't stay in the caverns. It was safe while they thought we'd been routed, when E-Gov thought the place was uninhabited. But once they know where we are…' She shuddered. 'I think Emrys is doing something. Something to keep us safe. Like Gwynne did.'

He peered at her, trying to make sense. 'I'm not sure I can take it all in, Anwen. I'm not sure what makes sense anymore. That little boy is certainly exceptional but he's still a child.'

Anwen smiled. 'Go and get some sleep if you can. I've a feeling it'll be another long day tomorrow.'

'Sleep! Now that would be something but I'm likely to toss and turn all night. I feel like I should be out there looking.'

'There are others out there and you've been out for hours already. Every area's being combed isn't it?'

'Yes but…'

'No buts. I'm speaking as your doctor now. Go to bed. Sleep. Do you want something to help?'

He shook his head. 'I'll do my best, doctor.'

Myrddin Emrys

I am Myrddin Emrys, druid, sorcerer and seer, who can shapeshift through space and time, cast illusions that convince. I am all of this and yet, in this life, I am a child. I cannot protect Y Tir alone. I cannot protect my mother without seeking help.

Her pain already resounds through my body, a prophecy I would rather not feel, but we are bound together. Others will care for her and I will be restored to her.

But every trauma leaves its print deep in the flesh. Already what she thought was my father's betrayal and then the implant—an early model, crude and toxic, have marked her body and soul, and now this new terror. But not for long.

I will return with more hope, more light in the enveloping dark.

7

Tomas woke to a faint knocking sound. He scurried out of bed, amazed that he'd slept finally, feeling disoriented as the wave of nausea at the thought of Emrys still lost crashed over him. He'd left Geraint with Angharad the day before and wished he could hold him. Hold his son and never let him go. He shook himself and opened the door.

'What the…'

Emrys ducked into the shack. Tall for an almost three year old, he was still visibly a small child and the incongruity of his knowing smile made Tomas long even more for his own boy, ordinary and easy.

'Emrys! Where…?'

'I'm afraid I can't tell you that,' Emrys replied. 'But I can tell you it's safe to leave the mines now. For everyone. They need to get back to their villages today. They'll be here by tomorrow so they need to stay indoors.'

'Emrys, slow down. I… Come and sit down.'

They sat facing one another, Emrys on a little wooden chair that Tomas had made for Geraint's fourth birthday. The last birthday Megan was alive to celebrate her son. He rubbed a hand across his forehead. 'How will it be safe in the houses? Can you tell me that?'

'Not exactly, only that the Regs from E-Gov won't see us.'

'And I can persuade people of this… How?'

Emrys grinned. 'Not going to be easy. You can convince them the mines are more dangerous. And they are. They'll use water, fire, explosives. All of the above. And the virus spreads more easily in the mines too.'

Tomas nodded. 'I told them as much last night before the meeting broke up in chaos when you went missing. There are people out there searching for you…'

'I know. I'm sorry about that. I needed to get help. Ifor will get to Oswestry tonight. It's not inhabited but there are guards there. He'll be giving them our whereabouts by this evening and he still has followers here. One in particular. I needed help to make sure we can move to the houses and not be seen. It's… it's more than I can manage on my own…'

'Maths and magic?'

'That's the way to think of it, yes.'

'And these followers? And this man? We have a…?'

'Sion Roberts,' Emrys said quietly, watching Tomas's face intently.

Tomas sprang to his feet as though something had bitten him. 'No! No, that's not… Sion? But Betsan…'

'Not Betsan. She has no idea.'

'But Sion… he…'

'Came to persuade you to join the committee, preferably to lead it?'

'Yes.' Tomas slumped back into his seat. 'I'm not up to this. Politics has never been my…'

'You are up to it, Tomas. They don't need politicians. You don't need to challenge Sion. Not yet. The main thing is to get people to move back to the villages.'

'The Regs will only go the caverns?'

'No, they'll be all over the place. In all the villages. Blaenau and Tanygrisiau especially, the places closest to Llechwedd and Cwmorthin. Perhaps they won't bother with Croesor and Rhyd. I'm not certain. But I can tell you they won't see us as long as we stay in the houses. We'll be hiding in plain sight.'

'I suppose there's no point asking how that'll be managed?'

'None at all.'

'And Sion?'

Emrys reached into a pocket and brought out a flash drive no bigger than the end of his toddler thumb. 'All the evidence about him is here, but there'll be time for that later. If it's needed. That's your decision.'

Tomas shook his head again. He got up and filled a kettle. 'I need some tea.' He busied himself for a few moments, adding herbs to a blue ceramic pot that Megan had treasured, before he added, 'I've got to give them some kind of explanation, though.'

'Of course. Okay. You tell them you've heard from Gerhard Raven. Myrddin's Mutineers have been tracking Ifor Tigean and were alerted when he left Y Tir. Their operatives have sent you a device. Top secret technology smuggled out of another vile regime in

Hungary. This thing generates an illusion that effectively makes buildings look empty of anything with a pulse. It can't work in open air. That's the story.'

'So it's not like whatever Gwynne Hughes used to protect the farms?'

'It doesn't actually exist, Tomas. It's just your cover story. Gwynne was simply… that powerful. I wish I could have met him.'

Tomas watches the child breathe in hard and wipe the corner of one eye but he doesn't comment.

'This… lets call it 'magic' for want of a better short-hand,' Emrys went on, 'this is going to take a lot of energy from a whole group of Mutineers, me included. I'm their link to the place. The indoor spaces concentrate the… well, let's just call it energy. The Regs will enter and see no-one.'

'I'm not sure they'll buy this.'

Emrys pointed to a sack by the shack door that Tomas hadn't noticed before. 'There's a huge number of tiny 'detonators' in there. There's nothing in them really but people like to have something tangible. Tell everyone to press the button as soon as they enter their houses and they'll be fine. Tell them they've all been double tested but there's enough for them to take two per house if it'll make them feel safer. Tell Anwen to take one too, in case someone notices.'

'Anwen? Why would she think she doesn't need one?'

'Because she already has the gift of invisibility, the ring of Eluned. She's another who is more than she seems.'

Tomas shook his head. 'I'm beginning to think I notice nothing. So that was how you and Sian disappeared from that angry meeting?'

'It was. But a story for another time. You need to call the meeting. Get things moving.'

'Yes, okay, but one other thing…'

'No.'

'Pardon?'

'You can't tell my mam I'm back. Not yet.'

'But I'll never persuade her to leave the cavern if she thinks you're still in there.'

'Tell her someone had a sighting of me walking towards the reservoir. Sion Roberts will back you up to get her to leave the mine. He wants us gone and he thinks the best ways is to hand us over to the Regs or let them find her in the village. He thinks the Regs will recognise his cover codes and let him and his family go with them to La-la land in E-Gov if he can just speak to them, but he knows that anyone left in the caverns will be wiped out and he wouldn't get his chance.'

Tomas shook his head again. 'I feel sick. And I still don't understand why Sian can't know you're safe.'

'I need to focus, Tomas. I need to concentrate more energy than I might even be capable of. I'm Myrddin Emrys, but I'm still three years old. If I have to deal with Sian… all that emotion… I hate her suffering like this, but… Once you get her out of the mine, tell her I've been found wandering the Moelwyns and I'm safe over in Croesor, taking cover in a house with the people who found me. Don't tell her too early in the day though, or she'll want to come after me.'

The boy looked like any small child, Tomas thought. He knelt down and hugged him. 'I understand. And thank you, Myrddin Emrys.'

Emrys sniffed away a stray tear and stood up. 'I'll actually be in your house in Tanygrisiau. Take my mam there with you and Geraint. Take Angharad and Gethin too, and Betsan and Sion. I'll be in the study. I can make a den under the old desk but keep them out of that room.'

Tomas nodded. 'Anything else?'

'Anyone from Croesor, Rhyd, Trawsfynydd and Maentwrog would be better off staying with friends until it's over. I doubt there will be drones watching the Moelwyns, but just in case. And anyway, it's quite a hike. Better to get everyone inside as quickly as possible. Stick to Blaenau as far as Llan, and to Tanygrisiau.

Tomas froze. 'But it's not just us. I mean… there are other communities. Beddgelert and Llanberis and on Anglesey…'

'The Mutineers have them all covered. You'll have to trust me on that. Ifor has contacts in some of those too, two contacts in Trearddur Bay. They were the main links to re-trading the supplies from Ireland. But we don't need to worry about any of that, I promise.'

He sounded like an adult in charge again, Tomas thought. He nodded and picked up the sack of fake detonators. 'Go well, Myrddin Emrys,' he said, and left his shack to this strange child who he was about to trust with all their lives.

Luned

And so we come to the battle. Over and over, the failure to balance the light and dark. The push of one to dominate the other. The lives lost in the space of that struggle.

Always there are betrayals. Always there are casualties. Always there are actions that could have been other, that lead to the resolutions and promises to change before the equilibrium is lost again.

And I will play my part, offer illusion and healing. I will wait with those I love and watch my daughter grow into the healer who will take on my mantle, becoming not only Gwen, sister of Emrys, but Gwenddydd, sister of Myrddin Emrys, of the house of Rhydderch Hael and Aurelius Ambrosius.

But first we must weather this conflict of light and dark, knowing that the world has always needed them both.

8

Tomas banged heavily on the table at his side. It had been set up on the platform in the assembly cavern, the members of the Gader ranged around it looking anxious. Slowly, the room came back to order, though murmurs continued. Sion Roberts got up from his seat on the far side of the table and moved to stand beside Tomas.

'We need to do as Tomas says and quickly. I know this is a lot to take in but we know Gerhard Raven from way back. We know his Mutineers are the best hope of freedom for so many of us. We couldn't have established Y Tir without them and if anyone can help us save it, it's them. The caverns have saved lives, but they've taken some of our finest people in the process.' He stopped to pat Tomas's arm. 'But now staying here could cost all our lives. We need to get out and quickly. A complete evacuation. Exactly as Tomas has outlined. We've got people out there already, looking for the little boy. The rest of us need to get out too.'

The atmosphere in the house was tense. When they arrived, Angharad had insisted on cooking for them all but they'd all picked at the food and promised to try again later.

The house smelt damp and Tomas noticed traces of mould around some of the windows. There was no electricity to make the ageing radiators work but there was wood in the storage tunnel behind the kitchen and he'd lit the stoves on the ground and middle floors. The upper one would heat water. A bath! How long since he'd soaked in a tub?

Dusk became darkness and they drifted from the kitchen to their rooms. Anwen had given Tomas herbs and pills for Sian, though now that he'd told her the boy was safe and in Croesor, she had stopped pacing and bursting into tears and was sleeping in the bedroom next to the bathroom, curtains drawn across both windows, Tomas's beloved books on the shelves. He'd missed them, many of them gifts from Megan. Geraint would sleep with him in the big room overlooking the garden and stream and Angharad and her grandson Gethin were in the blue room behind his, it's windows looking out on the overgrown track where the steam train had run until only a decade ago. Sion and Betsan were in the other big bedroom, on the floor below. He still couldn't take in the idea that Sion had been working with Ifor, betraying them, risking all their lives for money or for the mad dream of having a chip put into him by E-Gov.

Tomas stood looking out over the dark garden faintly lit by moon and stars. Would the Regs arrive tomorrow, the day after? Or would they come in the night? Tomas doubted anyone from the community would sleep tonight, despite the exhaustion they all must be feeling. But he was grateful when Geraint fell asleep after listening to three of the picture books they'd found in a box at the bottom of the bedroom shelves. They were books he and Megan had managed to get hold of before moving to the caverns, before Geraint was two. So many memories in the house.

It was dark when Tomas woke from half-sleep, groggy and confused, the sound of banging no longer in his dream but beneath him. He edged onto the landing and down the top stairs. Sion was already on the lower landing. He thought of telling Sion to go back into his room, but either the Mutineers' cover would work or it wouldn't. He let Sion follow him. There was banging in the kitchen and a voice with a Midlands accent grumbling that this was insane, a waste of time and resources.

'This place has been deserted for years, Guv,' another voice agreed. 'Look at those plates of food, manky with mould. They must've just up and left in the middle of dinner. Years ago by the looks of it.'

'Yeah and look at this old stove. It's only held together by rust. If anyone tried to light it, thing'd fall apart.'

Tomas and Sion exchanged puzzled glances as the door to the lower corridor was pushed open. The first of the three men stood facing them, looking through them.

'S'pose we'd better go round the whole place,' he said over his shoulder. 'We've come this far.'

'Yeah, s'pose we had. I thought they'd already been through this place, anyway, couple of years or more back. They didn't find anyone then and we're not going to now.'

The Regs passed Tomas and Sion and went upstairs towards the room that Betsan was in. They flung open the door and Tomas heard Betsan begin to scream, then swallow the sound.

'Empty,' called the man in the doorway, the thickset leader with close cropped dark hair. 'You two check the top floor.'

The others stomped past him, to where Sian, Angharad, Gethin and Geraint were sleeping in the three top storey bedrooms, though Tomas doubted they would be asleep after all the noise. He began to follow them, wanting to be in place to comfort Geraint, who would be confused despite having been told that some strange men might visit them, but not to worry.

'Hello,' Tomas heard Geraint say. 'My dad said…'

But the man had already left.

'Nothing in the other two rooms either,' his companion confirmed. 'Waste of time!'

They thudded downstairs, back towards the kitchen, passing Sion, who stood on the middle landing.

'Sion,' Tomas called from the top stairs. 'I know… I know you're…'

In the grey pre-dawn light, Tomas thought Sion's face flushed, but then he shook his head and said, 'I'm going to make sure they've gone, Tomas.'

Sion followed the Regs and Tomas heard the back door open.

'Sion! Don't…'

Tomas ran after them and Sion turned as he reached the outside door and shrugged, holding up both hands to Tomas before he walked outside.

Tomas sank onto the kitchen floor, his body shuddering.

'Hey, Regs, Regs, wait a… no need for that, I'm on your side…'

'Like hell you are,' one of the men spat back.

'Really, I'm with…'

The bang was ear-piercing. The window by the door rattled and Tomas heard a strangled half-sound before a thud. Sion's body falling, he thought, knowing it was useless to move.

'Well, who would have thought? Crighton, get in the car and alert all teams. Tell them to re-enter all houses. Look under beds, look in cupboards, lofts, behind curtains. Sneaky toads, these Welsh apparently. Griggs, get yourself back inside and start going through every room. And thoroughly. Filthy animals even left plates of mould to try to throw us off their scent. I'm going heft this one into the boot of the car. Evidence.'

Tomas stood, still shaking, as Griggs came back into the kitchen, red-faced, looking like he might be sick. Griggs pounded towards the stairs and Tomas followed as the Reg, an overweight man with puffy skin and high colouring, went back into Betsan's room. She sat on the edge of the bed, pale and shivering, as the man crawled beneath the bed and flung open the wardrobe, Tomas standing in the doorway trying to signal to stay calm.

'Why did they come back?' Betsan whispered, as Griggs moved upstairs, his footsteps followed by Crighton's and then their boss. 'And what was that noise? It was like fireworks, but… sharper… different.'

Tomas sat on the bed next to her. 'I need you to be brave, Betsan. I need… I have to fetch Angharad.'

He rushed up the stairs and watched the chief Regulator move into his own bedroom, before knocking on Angharad's door pushing it open. 'It's… Sion followed them out… he… Betsan needs you.'

'Did they shoot him?'

Tomas nodded. 'I'm sorry, Angharad, I…'

'Why did he follow them? We were told the shielding would only work if we stayed inside. Was he… He was betraying us, wasn't he?'

Tomas nodded again. 'Don't…'

'No, I won't tell my daughter that her husband died betraying us.' She brushed a hand through Gethin's mousy hair. 'Ah, to be innocent and sleep though it all.'

She got up and made for Betsan's room.

'We've seen too much loss, you and me,' she said quietly as she passed him.

Part 2

The Apprentice

9

May 2037

Angharad folded her arms and pursed her lips. 'You know, you could ask Emrys to help.'

The little boy, a small copy of Tomas Selwyn, though stockier than his wiry dad, flushed and crouched over the tablet he was punching at.

'Geraint?'

The boy shook his head. 'I want to do it myself.'

'Nothing wrong with that, but nothing wrong with getting some help either. We all need it from time to time.'

Gethin wandered over and sat next to Geraint. 'I couldn't work it out for ages myself,' he said casually, 'then it came to me that I just needed to think about it in more practical terms, like how many seeds to plant in an area or…'

'But you did it yourself, right?'

Gethin shrugged. 'Some of it, eventually anyway, but Nain got me started and then Emrys…'

'Mrs Parry's the teacher, not Emrys.' Geraint's colour rose again and he looked miserable. 'Emrys is younger than me.'

'Only a year. Gwen's two years younger than me, but she's better at maths than me, even though I'm getting into it more. And she knows everything about herbs and where all the bones are and…'

'Yeah, but her mam's a doctor.'

Gethin shrugged again. 'I'm told my dad could build anything and my mam was an amazing cook, but I'm not good at those. We're all just… we all have our own things.'

Geraint hunched further down in his seat. 'And Emrys's thing is being able to do everything.'

'Except kick a ball or catch one.' Emrys was stood beside Gethin. 'And I can't tell stories as well as you. But if you don't want me to help, why don't you ask Gwen?'

'She'll think I'm soft in the head.'

Angharad returned to Geraint's desk. 'Well, we've got quite a gathering here. Any progress on those percentages?'

Geraint shook his head.

'You know you don't have torture yourself with maths, Geraint. Taking a break can help too. Why don't you go out and do the weather readings for me? And take…' She looked around the classroom. 'Gwen!' she called. 'Could you give Geraint a hand with the weather readings?'

Gwen put down a tablet and nodded.

'And when you get back maybe you could do a history story with the little ones, or anyone who wants to listen for that matter?'

Geraint smiled. 'Yeah, I can do that.'

Angharad clapped her hands and knots of children who were scattered across the room ceased their activities and chatter to turn in her direction. 'Don't forget, it's a hot day today. Keep topping up your water. And if anyone wants a story, Geraint will be taking requests in about half an hour in the book room. Grab your floor cushion and enjoy.'

'Ready for weather duty,' Gwen said, smiling. She turned to Emrys and put an hand on his arm. 'How's your mam doing?'

Emrys nodded. 'A bit better. Your mam's been great.'

'Are you coming then?' Geraint asked gruffly.

Gwen smiled and nodded and followed Geraint outside to the weather station. Gethin shook his head. 'He looks like his dad. And he can tell stories like his dad. But boy, does he need to lighten up.'

'He will,' Angharad replied to her grandson. 'Staying for story time?'

Gethin grinned. 'I'm going to join Tomas and his crew in the forest near the lake. We're coppicing. Dewi's coming too.' Gethin paused. 'His dad's going to take Tomas's place on the council. Tomas's idea.'

Angharad nodded. 'Yes. I'll be at the meeting next week. He'll be good, I think.'

'But Tomas…'

'Like you were telling Geraint, we all have our strengths. Tomas Selwyn might be the calmest and most trustworthy man I've ever known, but he has no taste for politicking. They'll consult him anyway. Dafydd will do a good job. He listens long and speaks little and we're going to need…' She left the words hanging.

'Things aren't… Are we okay? I mean…'

'The trade with Ireland's been harder over the last year. Their new government is still finding it's voice, but it might turn out to be one we don't want to hear. But we've survived this long.'

Gethin nodded.

'Now, you get yourself going and while you're there, if the nettles aren't past their best yet, bring some back. We can make soup tonight.'

'Will do. There's tons of dandelions about if you want to make more vinegar or coffee. The leaves are getting a bit big and bitter for salads but they'd dry fine.'

'See what you can carry. Or you'll topple off your bike on the way home.'

Gethin grinned and turned to leave, waving across his shoulder as he reached the door.

Tomas gazed around the table at the group who had become known as the Gader, the gathering of those who made decisions for Y Tir, always with a great deal of listening to their neighbours. He watched them shaking their heads, several glancing around to see who would talk first.

'But we need you, Tomas. We wouldn't have got out of the mines without you. We'd have been drowned or burnt. And even in our own homes. It was you who got those… those detonators from Gerhard Raven.'

Tomas shook his head. He could insist it had all been down to a three-year-old boy, but Emrys was gradually blending into life in Y Tir. They wanted to forget anything 'strange' about him and, apart from his colour, which still bothered some of them, it was easier for them to think of him as an awkward eight-year-old, not the devil child that Ifor had tried to convince them had come to live in their midst.

'I've never been a politician. And it's been five years now. I've served my term. Dafydd's a better strategist than I'll ever be and I trust him. We need a strong negotiator to keep trade open with Ireland. And he's the right person for it. Between him and Betsan, we'll be well-served.'

Someone laughed. 'Keep it in the family, eh? We'll be toasting to the new power couple as well as to the baby at Jac's naming ceremony,' she added good-naturedly. 'Well, I for one am all for it. It's good to see Betsan having some happiness after what she went through and they've both got the gift of the gab for the Irish to respect. I vote we let Tomas get on with being the forester and farmer who makes sure we're not wholly reliant on the outside world.'

'Thank you, Seren.'

'I'll second that,' added Cen Talog. 'But they'll have their work cut out.'

There were nods and murmurs of agreement.

Tomas rapped gently on the table. 'So, I'll ask Betsan and Dafydd to come in shall I?'

'Yes,' Cen said for them. 'But I hope you'll stay for this meeting at least, Tomas. We could do with some input on how we're doing on food stocks and... the medicines too. I know Anwen and the others work miracles with herbs but there are some things...'

More nods and murmurs.

Tomas stood. 'Let me fetch in Betsan and Dafydd and I'll give you a report before I leave.'

When they had all resettled and Tomas had insisted on moving to the far side of the table, making space for Betsan to chair the rest of the meeting, Tomas began, 'I'm afraid it's not the best news by a long way...'

Later that evening, after Tomas had told a long tale of King Arthur to Geraint and was sitting at the kitchen table sorting seeds and humming to himself, there was an urgent rap on the door.

'Anwen, come in, you look...' He paused. 'Tea? Or do I need to fetch the whisky?'

She sat down heavily, opened her mouth to speak but only heaved a dry sob.

'Sian?'

Anwen nodded.

'Is Emrys...?'

'He's with Nain Parry. Him and Gwen. I wondered if I should leave them there tonight. I'm almost too tired to cycle to Rhyd, but...'

'Emrys has a way of sensing things?'

'Yes. Though hopefully he'll be asleep and might not…' She began to cry, fat tears and howling sobs. 'I'm so sorry, Tomas,' she said at last.

He handed her a clean tea towel, a piece of soft linen with a trail of red embroidered flowers. Megan had brought it back from their honeymoon in Szentendre, the small town not far from Budapest that had once been an artist's colony. The thought of Megan only sharpened his grief for Sian, for Emrys, losing his mother only weeks after his eighth birthday.

'I feel so responsible,' Anwen was saying.

'But you did everything you…'

'I could have done more if I'd had the right drugs. The skullcap and valerian worked well when she was more stable, but once the seizures worsened… even mistletoe wasn't strong enough in the end. Maybe for some it would have been, but Sian had… that implant had done so much damage before Gerhard got it out of her. It was one of the early ones, one of the…'

'Experimental models,' Tomas finished for her. 'All the more reason not to blame yourself. Sian had eight years with her son. Who knows how long she'd have had with that thing left in, even if she could have escaped the Regs looking for her.'

There was another knock at the door and both Anwen and Tomas startled. The handle moved and Gethin Parry burst in, out of breath and red-faced.

'Gethin! You're… sit down boy.'

Tomas gently pushed Gethin into a chair and Anwen stood to fetch water. 'Emrys?' Tomas asked.

Gethin gulped water and nodded. 'Nain went up to check he was asleep and he's gone. He was in my bed. I was going to have a mattress on the floor and Gwen's in with Nain, but she thought she'd better check he was okay before I went in, in case it would be better for me to sleep in the living room if he was having a bad night.'

'You cycled over here after working all day with us?'

Gethin nodded. 'I'm fine. I just went so fast. Nain told me to tell the Jenkins and a few others on the way so there's people out looking, but it's already getting dark.'

'Stay here with Anwen. You should both try to get some sleep. I'll raise a few others and start to look.'

Before Gethin could object that he should come too, Anwen said, 'No, you don't need to look for him. He'll have gone to Gerhard, to the Mutineers.'

Tomas and Gethin stared in silence.

'How do you…?'

'I just do.'

'Will he… will he come back?'

'I don't know, but I… I'm sure he's safe. And Gerhard will let us know.' She stood up, a little unsteadily. 'I'll ask Betsan and Angharad to help me tomorrow, with… to get Sian ready for the funeral. But I have to sleep now.'

She left the kitchen, making her way to the bedroom full of Tomas's beloved books, the room Sian and Emrys had slept in the first night that they'd left the mines five years earlier.

Blaise

And so my apprentice returns to me and the story will move on. Myrddin Emrys will grow into his power and the future will begin to move towards the coming again of Artu. This is how it will be, how it has always been, bringing the light of the Sun Child to this world again and again, but always the cost is high and in every generation Myrddin Emrys pays more than his share.

But we need the light in this terrible dark and so I will play my part.

10

It seemed like the whole of Y Tir turned out for the funeral. Everyone except her son, Tomas thought, as he stood at the head to the grave to begin the eulogy, but there… next to Anwen, Gwen tucked in close to her, there he was. Tomas made a tiny bow to Emrys. Could anyone else see him? Not everyone, Tomas thought, but a few. As Tomas began to speak, Gwen reached for Emrys's hand and squeezed it.

And then he was gone. Tomas scanned the thinning crowd. Would he ever see the child again?

In a stone hut in a forest, Gerhard sat on the end of Emrys's makeshift bed, watching the boy sleep at last. He looked up, disturbed by a slight noise at the living room door, to see Vivian hovering there. He put a finger to his lips and went into the corridor, pulling the door shut and lifting his daughter into his arms. She would be five in a couple of months, but weighed like air.

'Emrys's is sad,' she said.

Gerhard nodded. 'He's very sad, my love, but we'll take good care of him.'

Upstairs, he tucked her into her bed in the tiny second bedroom. 'Tell me a story,' she said sleepily, 'about Merlin.'

Gerhard stroked her head. 'Why Merlin?' he asked.

'Like Emrys,' she said simply.

He smiled and began the story, but she was asleep before he'd finished the opening and he crept out and into his own bedroom.

Lydie looked up from the book she was reading as he entered. 'Trying to distract myself,' she said. 'Is the poor mite asleep?'

He nodded. 'Exhausted after the funeral. He said his sister could see him. And Luned of course. But Tomas too, though he's not…'

'A wizard?'

Gerhard nodded again. 'Quite. Not a wizard, but he's formed a deep bond with the boy. And he's a natural bard. He keeps the history of Y Tir and back beyond it with ease. He's a good man.'

'Will Emrys stay with us now or will he return to Y Tir?'

'For now with us. There are things I can teach him and there's healing to be done. But he'll be needed there soon enough. He's always been needed there and will be for years to come. It's a complex life he has to negotiate. He needs to learn the skill his father had of…'

'Living two lives?'

'Yes.'

'And will that involve two families?'

'I think not.'

'Good. I don't want Vivian to have that to look forward to.'

Gerhard looked hard at his wife. An intelligent, beautiful, ordinary young woman from Burgundy, living near Huelgoat when he'd first met her. He was less and less sure of the 'ordinary' but more sure of his love each day. 'You think they'll…?'

'Myrddin Emrys, also known as Merlin, and Vivian. Of course they'll be together. Though not for quite some time. And then of course there's…'

'Morganne.'

'Quite.'

'Morfryn may have been a genius and your closest friend, but he certainly left quite a trail of fatherless children, and motherless too apart from Gwen.'

Gerhard nodded. 'Maybe he wouldn't have if Ygraine had lived. He was besotted with her.'

'Perhaps. Anyway, another half sister for Emrys to meet, but for now—' she leaned over and kissed him— 'we should both get some sleep.'

And so the apprenticeship of maths and magic began. A young man, François, dark-haired and laconic, taught him maths and programming while Gerhard taught him herbal knowledge, how to garden, build fires and cook, how to draw, paint and sculpt. Lydie, a historian and story-teller, like Tomas, and with the same way of gently observing people, passed on story after story.

'Watch Morganne. Relax. Watch carefully,' Gerhard said softly. 'I'll be back in an hour.'

Emrys breathed deeply and said nothing, but he turned towards his sister. She tossed dark curls away from her face and grinned. 'What do you want to be?'

'A falcon.'

'Of course you do. Okay. But today we're going to start with water. It's my element and I'll be a mermaid, but the change is the same principle. How about becoming a Zander? Weirdly, it's best to start with an element that isn't your strongest. But next time, or maybe the one after, you can show me your falcon. I'll be a raven and fly with you. Ready for the river?'

Emrys hesitated.

'What?'

'The tincture… will I…?'

'Once you're adept you won't need it.'

'Okay and…'

'You won't need anything except yourself. It's all in you, Emrys. The tincture, the pentagram, the river weed or whatever you're using… they embody what's in you already. It's like learning the tightrope. Once you're confident, you can take away the net.'

Emrys looked up. Through the water he could see Morganne, a mermaid sitting on the bank of the river, her tail splashing him so that he was constantly washed sideways. She jumped in, giggling and the ripples propelled him downstream.

'Swim, Emrys, swim!' Morganne's voice sounded louder, clearer under the water. He began to flick his fins, his whole body undulating, moving him forward. He dived deeper, then rose again through green water, which he gulped down to fuel the next shimmy.

He heard Morganne laugh, the noise sharper in the river, then, 'Emrys! Emrys!'

He flicked around to see a large perch heading towards him, grey strips against its yellow-green scales, gulping fast.

'Go to the bank! Quickly! Go to the bank! You need to change…'

Emrys panicked and dived deeper, hearing Morganne scream above him. The water was muddier near the river bed. He gulped hard and flipped again, unable to orient for a moment. The perch was above him, closer and there was a larger shadow behind it.

'Morganne!'

The perch gulped harder, harder, trying to escape the creature pursuing it.

Emrys swam towards the bank, leapt and… was on the earth, wet and breathless, a nine-year-old boy in the July sun.

Morganne surfaced, did a leap and landed on her feet on the grass next to him.

'So, how are you getting on with your sister now?' Gerhard asked as they walked back through the forest to the Raven's cottage.

The first few months, Morganne had been distant with him. She was polite and aloof. Perhaps it was simply that a fourteen-year-old didn't suddenly want to have a younger brother, he'd thought. But towards the end of his first year with the Mutineers, Gerhard had drawn Morganne into teaching him and she warmed to the task.

'She's… kind of fierce, but… clever and funny. I mean, it's not like she tells jokes, but you can see she has this…'

'Mischief in her?'

'Yes.'

'And you like that?'

Emrys nodded.

'Good. People don't always find her easy and I realise she's taken her time to decide to like you. She can be charismatic in her way, but she's intense too. And not the most flexible of youngsters. She knows her mind and there's not a lot of changing it. I'm glad you like her.'

'I can't believe I really did that. I mean… even though I can… travel… you know, like I did when Y Tir was going to be over-run by the Regs and I needed to get to you in an instant. Somehow, that's always felt ordinary to me, but changing shape felt so much more… strange and difficult, I suppose.'

'But you did it. The shamanic arts usually come much later in the apprenticeship, but with you… Well, a lot of what we are doing is re-awakening your skills rather than teaching them for the first time. So there's a lot coming at you at once.'

'It's weird. It all feels new until I do it once and then it's like it's been there forever. Except the maths and IT. That just feels new.'

'I suppose that's because it is. You and François are working at the boundaries of theory, continuing your father's work, but François tells me you work as though you already know it.'

Emrys grinned. 'It just seems natural. Once I get into it. It just…'

'Flows?'

'Yes.'

They walked on in companionable silence, but as they neared the cottage Emrys asked, 'Will I go back to Y Tir?'

'What do you think?'

'I think I will. I think that's what the maths is for. But the art… I love it. But I'm not sure where it fits.'

Gerhard grinned. 'Could be for its own sake.'

Emrys nodded. 'And yet I think…'

'You're right. You will go back to Y Tir and protect them with your maths and magic, and make trade deals using the products of it, so they can have food and medicines. But you will have a second life too.'

'Like Morfryn?'

'Exactly.'

'But… I don't want to have different children who don't even know about each other and… and their mams…' he trailed away, red-faced and breathless.

'Then you won't. And I'm glad of that. But Y Tir will come first. We'll go on with the art while you're here. But then you'll have to teach yourself for a few years while you practise not only travelling but something that falls between the travel and shapeshifting. We'll both know when you're ready. At that point, you'll begin to move between two worlds and in each you will look different. More like Morfryn in E-Gov territory where you'll become my art apprentice. More like a darker version of Sian in Y Tir.'

'When... when can I go back?'

'Another four years maybe. After that you'll be able to spend time here occasionally to go on learning but you won't need to live with us. I know that seems like a long time but once druid apprenticeships once lasted much longer than five years. This is the express version. Do you miss Y Tir a lot?'

'Yes,' Emrys said quietly. 'You were right about there being good people there. I miss Anwen, Gwen and Tomas a great deal. But others too, Nain Parry and Gethin. I even miss Geraint. He could be so... grumpy, but not always and... It's not that I don't like it here—this place is... well, magical, but... it's like I belong in Y Tir, even though I was an outsider at first.'

'The years will fly by,' Gerhard promised.

And so they did.

Myrddin Emrys

What if there are places where the dream is what is real? In the forest in Brittany, I learnt to see through the appearance of things. The illusions of this age are politics, religion, law. The forest knows other realities. A new artwork hangs in the spray above a waterfall, in the light between trees, on the path between the vaulted branches that make a temple of the woods.

Their vast arches are shelter and solace from a world running on insanity. There are no clocks here, only the dappled sunlight changing to moonlight, leaves changing colour, the voice of the water. In the forest, trees stand guard over decades, their branches raised like the antlers of great stags. The massive oak, Hètre du Voyageur, may be the sprit of the stag-god, Cernunnos, holding a threshold between worlds.

But it is not a threshold I can cross, and could not even when my mother had gone beyond it.

11

September 2042

Emrys hugged Lydie one last time and Vivian began to sob. Gerhard leaned down and hugged her. She was almost ten, the age Emrys had been when he arrived in Brocéliande, but she looked younger, fine-boned and fragile, though he knew she was stronger than she looked.

'Emrys will be back,' Gerhard consoled. 'He'll visit us often.'

'It won't be the same though,' she said, sniffing and breathing hard.

'I know, sweetheart. It won't be the same. But Emrys has work to do in Y Tir. And one day…'

Lydie shot him a look and he knew she was right. It was best not to tell people their future. Best not to know at all. And he didn't, not in detail. But he knew that one day Vivian and Emrys would be more than childhood friends.

Emrys stood awkwardly. 'I'll miss you too,' he said quietly.

Vivian nodded emphatically. 'Of course you will. I'm the best thing about the forest.' She grinned. 'Visit often?' she asked.

'I promise.'

She nodded, looking sad again, but said, 'Go well, Myrddin Emrys Hughes, who will one day become Nazir Malik.'

They stared at her.

'What? You can all be prophets, but I'm supposed to be just a kid?'

Gerhard laughed. 'That's my girl. Now, we should really be going.'

Gwen took Emrys's hand and pulled him into the house. Around the table people looked up.

'What's he doing here?'

It was Geraint who spoke. Emrys looked across at the boy who'd always been uneasy with him, flushed and grown both taller and broader in his absence.

Geraint shrugged. 'I meant, when did you get back?'

'Well, that's what the surprise is, then. Wow!' Gethin came towards him and embraced him, slapping him on the back and the room erupted into questions and greetings.

He was glad to see them, even Geraint. Gerhard had taken him to Anwen's house the evening before. It was only when Anwen opened the door, fully prepared for who would be there, that he realised she too was one of the wizards, was not only who she seemed to be. He wondered about his own mother. Morfryn had chosen Ygraine and Gwynne had chosen Anwen, who was also Eluned. Both women were more than they appeared to be. But Sian had been… just his mam. He still couldn't think about her without tears pricking at his eyes but perhaps Anwen and the others would think it was just overwhelm at being back.

He looked around the room again. Tomas waved to him from the stove where he was cooking up a feast with Betsan. Angharad waited for her grandson to finish his back-slapping and then hugged Emrys tightly. Dafydd Jenkins stood and shook his hand and Dewi repeated Gethin's ritual.

Emrys blinked and looked around again. Gethin and Dewi must be fifteen now and Geraint fourteen, a year older than him and Gwen. A little girl of about three emerged from under the table and handed him a knitted cat.

'Meow,' the little girl said. She was the image of Betsan, but… Dewi swung her into his arms and onto his shoulders and the girl giggled, gripping his unruly hair for stability.

'Ow, Ceri, you monkey.'

She laughed harder. 'Meow,' she said again, reaching towards Emrys.

'That's the name of her toy cat,' Dewi said. 'Emrys, meet my little sister.'

Emrys smiled and handed the cat up to Ceri. So Betsan must have married Dewi's dad, another widower from the years of virus and caverns.

'Sit down,' Anwen said. 'Food will be soon. And we'll try not to ask a million questions all at once.'

Tomas put a large pan of sweet-scented root veg onto the big trivet on the table. 'Anwen's been telling us all this time she was sure you were safe. I'm glad she was right.'

Betsan set down a second pot of stew and smiled warmly. 'Welcome home, Emrys,' she said simply. 'Dewi, Gethin, can you fetch some more bottles of kombucha from the tunnel?'

The teenagers disappeared into the kitchen area and returned with swing top bottles that fizzed when opened, the sour-sweet amber liquid going perfectly with tender carrots and beets, soft dumplings and broth.

He was exhausted by the time the party began to disperse. He told stories all evening. Stories of Gerhard, Lydie and Vivian, of Morganne, who swam like a mermaid, though he didn't mention that she was his half-sister, just as he was careful not to hint that Gwen too was his sister, stories of the forest and the trees, animals and birds, though he didn't mention soaring above it on falcon wings.

When most had left for their own homes, Tomas put a hand on his shoulder. 'You know we've got plenty of space here. You'd be welcome to live with us if you'd like to.'

He glanced at Geraint, who flushed and looked at the table, and was glad to notice Anwen shaking her head.

'We're a bit tighter on space but Emrys is family. He should be with us.'

Geraint looked up and Emrys could almost hear the questions forming in his mind, but he didn't ask them out loud.

Anwen smiled towards Geraint, as though she sensed the same thing. 'Well, Sian was a Hughes like my Gwynne,' she said.

Geraint nodded. 'Oh, yes. Yes, I see.'

He sounded defeated, Emrys thought, watching Geraint watch Gwen as she pulled on a coat against the evening's soft rain. He doesn't want me here, living with him and Tomas, but he doesn't want me living with Gwen either. It'd be kinder to tell him we're brother and sister but hard to explain.

Everyone knew he was the son of Morfryn Nazir Malik and Sian Hughes.

Emrys smiled. 'Thanks for offering though, Mr Selwyn.' He turned to Geraint. 'Fancy a walk up to Dinas Emrys some time? I've really missed that place.'

Geraint returned his smile. 'Yeah, that'd be good. We can tell the Vortigern story.'

Emrys nodded. 'You're on.'

Gwenddydd

And so he clung to me, my brother, tortured by loss and by his gifts of prophecy. He knew the secrets of things, the motion of the stars, the flight of birds, the gliding of fishes and when his muse possessed him he could be prey to wild ideas, but he knew little rest. His quasi-omniscience was as much affliction as gift.

In Y Tir only my mother, Anwen, and Tomas knew that we shared a father. My father, Gwynne Rhydderch Hughes, another who was more than he seemed, and Morfryn Nazir Malik, appeared to be two unrelated men who died on the same day in far apart places. My father's horse slipped down a bank in Tanygrisiau and he drowned, knocked unconscious by a rock he hit as he fell. He died as Rhydderch Hael, king of the north, had died in a previous life when Merlin's sister was his wife, not daughter. In each generation the story shifts its details yet things remain the same.

Morfryn died on a road out of Brocéliande. The agents of E-Gov had failed to find their way in, but they laid in wait. They were one soul and so died in the same moment.

Everyone knew the co-incidence that Emrys and I were born on the same day, but not that both of us were wizards, me of healing, coming more slowly into my powers and consciousness, and he of prophecy and maths, shapeshifting and illusion.

12

October 2043

They walked across the tops, coming down into Beddgelert and following the tree-lined river. It was a bright October day, the sky blue, sun radiant but cool, a smattering of copper and amber leaves still on the trees, others scrunching underfoot.

They walked though the village and out towards the woodland with its magical pool before the low hills rose towards the path leading to the summit of Dinas Emrys, from where they could see the sweep of Snowdonia across the lake and all the way to Yr Wyddfa, already tipped in snow.

They were quiet as they walked but at the top they sat on the edge of the ruined tower walls and Geraint began the story of Merlin and Vortigern while Gwen unfolded waxed sheets containing thick cheese sandwiches and apples. It was a story they knew well but could hear over and over, of how Vortigern's tower collapsed night after night as two dragons woke and fought. Of how he sacrificed children in an attempt to keep the tower standing until the child, Merlin, challenged him with the truth.

When Geraint had finished, they ate and gulped down water.

'Now the dragons are technologies,' Emrys said finally.

'What do you mean?' Geraint asked.

'The red dragon is us. The white dragon is E-Gov. To keep our tower standing we have to defeat them by being better at maths and magic.'

Geraint's brow furrowed. 'Magic?'

'Just a saying. We have to beat them at their own game. Out-manoeuvre their technology.'

'It's political alliances we need,' Geraint countered, 'not tinkering with computers. And we should fight them if it comes to it. Plant bombs, sabotage, whatever it takes.'

Gwen shook her head and Geraint flushed.

'Only if there's no other way to stay safe, I mean. I…'

'You can't win the peace with war,' Gwen said, her voice quiet but determined.

'No, I mean…' Geraint reached for another sandwich and hunched down, eating.

'Emrys is right,' Gwen added.

Geraint's colour rose and his eyes flashed. He opened his mouth but Emrys spoke first. 'But Geraint's right too. We do need alliances. They're crucial. Y Tir can't keep going without them and people who can play politics and negotiate alliances give us more protection and make a big difference.'

Geraint smiled at him and nodded emphatically. 'Yeah, Dafydd's brilliant at that stuff. I think Dewi will be too. He's already really good at getting into a situation and making it… just making it smoother somehow.'

'I think you'd be good at it too,' Emrys added.

Geraint flushed even redder and hunkered into his sandwich.

'Yes, you would,' Gwen agreed. 'Not my thing at all.'

'But you'll be a doctor like your mam. You're already helping. Dad says you're really gifted.'

It was Gwen's turn to smile broadly. 'So, we've all got our talents,' she said. She stood and flicked crumbs from her sweater. 'Race you to the bottom of the mound.'

She set off at speed before the two taller boys could stand, but they easily overtook her, the three of them panting hard as they collapsed, laughing, by a gnarled rowan tree.

On the way down, Gwen stopped by the pool. 'I'm going to sit a while,' she said. 'I've got my journal with me. I'll catch up with you in the village.'

The boys nodded and wandered on, walking slowly, quiet at first.

'Gwen's like…' Geraint began. 'I mean you and Gwen. You're…'

'Like sister and brother?'

'Pardon?'

'You were saying, me and Gwen are like sister and brother.'

'No, I... I mean I thought... I thought she might. I mean she really looks up to you and...'

'Believe me, as far as I'm concerned, we *are* brother and sister.'

Geraint's smile was the most radiant Emrys had ever seen. 'That's great. I mean...'

'It's fine, Geraint. Gwen likes you too.'

'She does?'

Emrys shoved Geraint good-naturedly and Geraint returned with a mock headlock. They tussled their way along the street until they came to the bridge, where they sat on the wall waiting for Gwen in companionable silence.

'Don't forget, no unnecessary risks.' Dafydd glanced around the group, faces a mix of eagerness and anxiety. 'You've got a tablet in each pair so Emrys can monitor your movements. Keep it on quiet mode and only use it if essential. Emrys will be in the van and can give you directions on your ear-pieces if needed. You've got passes that mimic their tags to get you in and they act as ID. You know the routes from the run-throughs. Keep calm. Get to your targets, pick up and get out. Any questions?'

All of them looked more anxious now, Emrys thought, as they nodded agreement with Dafydd. Adrenaline and training would see them through, he told himself. And his maths and magic. Gethin looked the most calm. Dewi and Geraint were flushed and moved constantly, full of nervous energy. Lowri and Rhian seemed more subdued.

His friends were going into a medical supplies depot across the border of E-Gov, not far into South Wales, but far enough that everyone there was recognised by the tag implanted in them. And their safety was down to him. Gerhard had insisted he was ready to do it alone. The 'passes' he'd given out were placebos. They would enter the facility and appear to be tagged, the same as any E-Gov citizens with clearance, but only so long as he was making it happen.

A wave of nausea swept through him and he realised Dafydd was shepherding them towards the van.

There'd been other raids. Animal stock or small food depots on the edge of the Subs where the people weren't tagged. Emrys hated those urban wildernesses, the people working at menial tasks invented as a means of population control, subsisting on diets of processed food and false information, constantly hoping to win a lottery or earn a promotion to be tagged and become an E-Gov citizen. The food plants they raided were cold stores of vegetables or grains that would never be eaten by people in the Subs so at least they weren't stealing from those already living wretched lives. The raids into the Subs were still dangerous. There were armed guards and tight surveillance, but nothing on the level of medicine warehouses, which were never in the Subs and which they'd never had to raid previously.

But another change in regime in Ireland had cut off their supplies once more. Emrys took his seat in the van and sighed.

'You okay?' Geraint asked.

Emrys pulled himself out of his thoughts. 'Yeah, just thinking.'

'Ah, that way madness lies,' quipped Geraint. 'But you've got this covered, right?'

Emrys nodded. 'Yeah. I have.' He forced himself to sound confident. 'I was more thinking about how it would be great to get some stability with the trade deals so we wouldn't have to do this kind of thing.'

Gethin turned from the seat in front of him. 'But you're onto it, right?'

'I've got some ideas. Something I'm working on that they might want so much they won't care whether our politics align with their latest slogans.'

'Good. And you've got our backs today. So don't beat yourself up. You're doing everything you can.'

'I suppose, but there's got to be a better way.'

Alone in the van, Emrys sat on the floor and let the outside world fall away. It might have been better to go for invisibility, he thought. No. Don't second-guess yourself. They're about to be in there, relying on you. He let the babble in his mind go and a felt a buzz of clear focus jolt him. They were in, quickly and quietly. Three pairs heading in different directions. He sensed each heartbeat.

'Hey, do I know you? You new or…'

He heard Gethin laugh lightly. 'What you talking about?' His voice had taken on a different lilt, more southern. 'We were on stock duty all last week together, mate.'

'Yeah, of course, don't know what came over me then. Actually, I'm feeling a bit off today. Sort of weird. Think I might…' The man turned away from Gethin and Rhian and wandered in the other direction.

'Good,' Emrys whispered into their ear-pieces. 'You're doing great.'

Dafydd and Geraint had already reached their target. All clear and quiet. They began loading their backpacks. Emrys breathed evenly, felt the energy flowing from him in waves.

Dewi and Lowri were about to enter their target room.

'That store's off-limits. New order.'

Emrys steadied his breath. They can handle this, he told himself.

'Special order,' Lowri said. 'We're…'

'Ifor?'

What? Why had Dewi said that?

'You knew my brother?'

No! Emrys's mind flipped. Keep control.

'Distract him, Lowri,' Emrys whispered.

'Well, that's a co-incidence,' Lowri began, voice even-toned and warm. She's good at this, Emrys thought. 'Dave here has a brother called Ifor. You sound just like him. Your brother an Ifor as well?'

'Was. My brother *was* called Ifor.'

'Sorry, mate,' Dewi joined in. 'Like Laura said, my brother's got your exact voice. Weird, eh?'

Emrys focussed tightly. They were doing fine.

'More than weird. Not the only thing that's weird. For a minute there, it was like you weren't connected… You seemed…'

'Anyway, best be getting on with this. High level order.'

'Yeah, right. But let me just check something.'

'We're on the clock here, mate…'

'Best let me do my job then,' Ifor's brother retorted. The three stood in silence, Ifor's brother staring at them intently. 'Okay. Laura Davies?'

'That's me.'

'You look… young for your age.'

Lowri smiled. 'I get that a lot.'

'Yeah? We should go for a drink sometime.'

'That'd be great. You've got my mind link. Message me—anytime.'

'And Dave Jones? Yeah. Think we worked on a job together a couple of weeks back.'

'Yeah? Memory like a bucket of holes, me. Anyway, we should…'

'Of course. Hope to see you soon, Laura.'

'You too.'

The pair ducked inside the door, which slid open for them.

Dewi held tightly to Lowri as they leant on the closed door. 'Wow! I had no idea Ifor had a brother working for E-Gov. He…' Lowri paused.

'…must have been Ifor's contact for fencing our supplies.' Dewi finished for her. 'So that guy knows Y Tir is real. I don't even want to think about it, cariad. Let's get the medicines and get back to the van.'

'Yeah, I was okay when we were facing him but I feel really shaky now.'

'Me too,' said Dewi, already loading his backpack and holding out a hand to take Lowri's.

Back in the van, Emrys exhaled. 'I have to do something better than this,' he said out loud a moment before Gethin and Rhian opened the van door, Dafydd and Geraint close behind them.

Dafydd shot an enquiring look at Emrys. 'They're fine. They ran into someone asking questions, but they handled it.'

'Questions?'

'The store they were targeting had a new security rating and…'

Dafydd waited.

'And the guy who stopped them was Ifor Tigean's brother.'

'No! Iwan?'

Emrys focussed to scan the depot's security rosta. 'Yes.'

'But Iwan… He was supposed to have died in the last wave of pandemic, back in '28. Him and Ifor were twins. They must've…'

'Planned to get one of them into E-Gov early on so they could make money selling Y Tir's supplies.'

'All that time.' Dafydd shook his head. 'Unbelievable! Is Ifor…'

It was Emrys's turn to shake his head. 'No, Ifor didn't make it. But here come Dewi and Lowri.'

Dafydd started the van as they piled in. 'Well done, all of you. Now let's get this stuff safely back to Anwen.'

Myrddin Emrys

And so I will become both apprentice and teacher and the cycles will continue, as they always must. It is hard to leave Y Tir again but I know I must act, that I must be able to do something better than supporting raids against E-Gov, letting my friends take terrible risks. It is time to come into my powers more fully and while I learn from Blaise, Vivian will become my apprentice, as she always must. Vivian, the lady of the lake, endowed with the spirit of Eluned the Fortunate, as Anwen also is. Vivian will soon outstrip me as she always does.

Together we will usher in the time of the light, the time of Artu. But first there is much to endure, joy and grief. And while I learn from Blaise and mentor Vivian, my sisters' powers wax with each day. Already Morganne is adept in illusion and justice and Gwenddydd becomes a more magical healer with each moon's passage. In every life it is Gwenddydd who steps in when the burdens of prophecy and power become too heavy. My quiet, watchful sister, who makes herself seem so ordinary, without whom so many would not survive.

13

Emrys freed himself from Vivian's embrace, laughing. 'Okay, monkey, enough, while there's still some breath left in me.'

She grinned and let go. 'I'm not a monkey. I'm a mermaid like Morganne.'

Emrys smiled at her. 'Of course, my lady of the lake,' he added.

'Except Morganne won't teach me. She says I have to be twelve but she's making it up.' She stopped to pretend to pout, then went on, 'But you can teach me. I'll be your apprentice. You will, won't you?'

'I…'

'So, you're ready for the next part of the work?' Gerhard asked, coming into the small living room.

'I am.'

'And he's going to teach me to shift,' Vivian added.

Gerhard raised his eyebrows but offered no comment except, 'Well, you mustn't monopolise him. He's got a lot to learn in a short time.'

'But you'll stay for Solstice?'

Emrys looked towards Gerhard, who nodded. 'But not much longer than that. I'll let Lydie know you're here and François. He'll be delighted. I want to teach you some of the light art too. Eventually, the two will come together, but…'

'Me too. Will you teach me too?'

Gerhard pursed his lips. 'We...ll...'

'I'm so bored. You know maman is expecting a baby? She's huge and tired all the time.'

Emrys laughed. 'Not much longer now, though.'

'No, but she won't have loads of time for me when she's got a baby to look after! I don't mind though... I'm looking forward to seeing my sister.'

'You know it's a girl?'

Gerhard smiled. 'Only Vivian knows.'

'Ah.'

'She *is* a girl. Anyway, can I learn too?'

'Yes, but you have to let me concentrate on Emrys. He needs to learn fast.'

Vivian threw her arms round her father. 'I promise! Thank you.' She turned back to Emrys. 'Now, about that shapeshifting.'

The Yule log was left at the cottage door. Earlier, Gerhard and Emrys had left logs at other doors and helped to haul in the huge body of a fallen oak to the communal barn where the celebrations always began before people went back to their cottages in family groups or with friends. But first they had carried jugs of wine through the forest, pouring libations for the fruiting trees as they sang wassailing carols.

The communal rituals over, they gathered around the laden table in the cottage kitchen, Lydie easing herself into a wooden armchair, Vivian full of energy.

Gerhard filled glasses with red wine, adding water to Vivian's, and pouring a steaming jug of Venus Rob into his pregnant wife's glass in place of alcohol. While Gerhard filled glasses, Vivian placed a fragrant beeswax candle in front of each of them. The lights were extinguished and, in the darkness, Gerhard said, 'We come together for Alban Arthan. May the light of Artu be reborn in us as it is in Mabon, the Sun Child returning.'

'May the light of the constellation of the Great Bear lead us through the dark winter, back to Artu's light,' Lydie took up the response.

'May the Divine Child be born in each of us, to warm the earth and bring new life,' Vivian said solemnly.

'And may the Light of Winter, the Light of Artu, be with us as the seasons turn, and always,' Emrys finished.

A chair scraped and Emrys, his eyes adjusting to the thick, soft darkness, could dimly make out Gerhard's shape bending to the fire. There was the sound of striking and a small flame, held to a remnant of last year's Yule log, burst yellow and amber in to the dark. Gerhard opened the woodburner and tucked the lit twig into kindling carefully arranged beneath the oak log, a gift from a neighbour and from the forest. He lit a taper from the budding blaze and carried it around the table, lighting each of their candles.

'The light to you,'

'And also to you.'

When Gerhard was seated again, Vivian stood and fetched a trail of mistletoe from a side table decorated in greenery. She put a small piece of mistletoe before each of them, sat and raised her glass.

'May Druidh-lus bring you inspiration this year.'

They each raised a glass and sipped. Then Emrys took up the toast. 'May Druidh-lus bring you healing this year.'

Lydie went next. 'May Druidh-lus bring you guidance this year.'

Finally, Gerhard added, 'May Druidh-lus bring you fertility this year.' He smiled at his wife, who blew him a kiss. 'And now, food!'

They sat at the table long into the evening, enjoying the feast, telling stories, sharing their fears and hopes for the coming year.

'Well, I, at least, must sleep,' Lydie said. 'Thank you, all. I can't ever remember a Solstice without cooking.' She pulled herself up, resting the palms of her hands on the small of her back and rubbing. 'Oh!' She stepped back as though to escape the puddle appearing at her feet. 'Oh, my…' She laughed. 'A Solstice baby! Emrys, can you fetch Armelle?'

Emrys picked up a lantern and set off for the midwife's cottage, following a familiar track lit by the waning gibbous moon, bright in the field of stars above the winter trees.

He was back with Armelle in less than an hour but already the labour was advancing. Gerhard looked white and he noticed Vivian hovering in the corridor beyond the kitchen, looking anxious.

Armelle was brisk and kind, taking charge, allotting tasks.

'Vivian. I want you to go and stay with François and Enora for tonight. Do you want Emrys to walk you?'

She shook her head then opened her mouth. Emrys thought she would protest but the wail from her mother made her freeze, colour draining from her. 'You'll take care of her.'

'I will,' Armelle agreed.

'I don't need anyone with me. I… I'll just get a coat and put some things in a bag.'

'Thank you. Emrys, I need you…'

When Emrys woke, there was a moment when he wasn't sure where he was, or what time it might be, before the images flooded back. Vivian! Had anyone told Vivian? Of course they would. Of course Armelle…

He struggled out of bed and down to the kitchen. The fire was cold and the room icy. Gerhard took his head out of his hands and looked up. 'Sorry, I should…' He glanced around the room, dazed, not sure what it was he should be doing.

'No. I'll make tea. I… Has anyone…?'

'Armelle went to see Vivian at François and Enora's.' He paused and breathed deeply. 'Lydie was so strong, Emrys. So full of life. And the baby. She looked… she was so prefect. Innogen… we were going to call her Innogen.'

'I'm so sorry,' Emrys whispered.

'Vivian will be back soon. I… I don't know what to say to her…'

'That Lydie loved her.'

Gerhard nodded and began to weep.

Vivian sniffed back tears. 'I wish you'd stay longer.'

'I know. I wish I could too but it's already been an extra month and…'

She nodded. 'Go well, Myrddin Emrys.' She threw her arms around him.

'And you…' He paused. 'That ring… it's…'

'It was maman's. Papa gave it to me yesterday.'

'But it's…' He looked towards Gerhard.

'It's not the same as it was with Morfryn and Gwynne,' he told Emrys. 'They were two aspects of one person and you will learn to do that in time. But with Lydie and Anwen, each of them is, or was, an aspect of Eluned, though separate people, and the ring exists for each of them.'

'Eluned blends with the forest and finds her way in the Otherworld of Annwn,' Vivian added quietly.

'Yes. And guards the hidden fountain of Barenton where Merlin first met Vivian,' Emrys added, smiling. 'You do know that ring…'

'Is powerful and can allow me to become invisible? Yes. And no, before you ask, I don't think it's a toy.'

'Sorry. Of course.' He hugged her quickly again and turned to the door, not daring to look back.

Gwenddydd

And so my brother will return, his powers at their height, ready to defend Y Tir from the darkness of extinction another time. He will win their trust with maths and magic and they will feel again the strength of the red dragon and rejoice. But our enemies too will sense the power of Myrddin Emrys and so his success will also hasten the forces of darkness in massing against us again. This constant rhythm of quiet and conflict, darkness and light.

But afterwards, perhaps for a little while, a time of stability, a time of healing. That will be my time, a time to build and heal.

14

October 2044

Emrys sat to the side of Dafydd at the meeting of the Gader. He still felt uncomfortable at these gatherings. Y Tir had had a good year and everyone in the room recognised that was largely down to him. At last the red dragon was proving itself better at maths and magic, thanks to all he'd learnt in Brocéliande. But still, their life was so fragile and he felt so responsible for it all.

'The ships arrive this weekend,' Dafydd told them. We need everyone who can make it to be on Ynys Môn ready to transport, fill stores and distribute. This should be the best winter we've had in a very long while. And we have Emrys to thank for that, which is why I asked him to be at the meeting today.'

The murmurs were all of approval but Emrys felt a shiver run through him. 'I've only been able to do this because of all I was taught by Gerhard and others in Brocéliande,' he said. 'And we have to stay vigilant, they…'

'Yes,' Iolo Evans agreed. 'They've put up more border controls to the south and east. We're highly dependent on this new arrangement with Ireland and the regime there is otherwise sympathetic to E-Gov. They're only trading with us because they need Emrys's technology, but—and no offence, Emrys, I think what you're doing for us is brilliant—it wouldn't take much to change the wind.'

'Iolo's right,' Emrys agreed. 'I have to stay well ahead of anything E-Gov can offer them instead. It'd be better if there was someone who could work with me, but…'

'How about Gethin?' Elen Griffith asked.

Gethin shook his head as those round the table turned in his direction. 'I'm good enough at maths for most purposes, but not the stuff that Emrys is juggling to write those programmes. That's like magic to me.' He grinned at Emrys.

'I don't mean to worry you. I can keep going and the latest deal will get us through the winter. It's not that I've got any immediate worries, but looking ahead… I'll talk to Gerhard about it. I'm going to need to visit the forest in the New Year.'

Dafydd patted him on the back. 'We appreciate everything you're doing, and we know it's a lot of responsibility. You've already done wonders and no one can control all the variables. You're a miracle as far as I'm concerned. E-Gov must have thousands of their drones working on writing code and yet the Irish want yours.'

'Yes, but it makes us vulnerable too. E-Gov might tell its citizens we don't exist and they might not have been able to locate us so far, but they definitely know we're here. My programmes bring in food, but they put us on the map too.'

It was Rhys Ellis who answered this time. 'We've been talking about that, lad. You're absolutely right. Bit of a tightrope walk, isn't it? But if we don't trade then we almost starve and go without medicines. Or we're forced to launch raids that put those making them at terrible risk, often young people. We figured E-Gov will be getting more interested in us again if they think we're doing well so we wondered if your friends in the Mutineers would equip us with those cloaking detonators again. The ones Gerhard issued to us back in '32.'

Emrys nodded. 'Yes.' He hesitated. 'Thing is, they… they take a lot of energy. Making them was… The Mutineers put everything they had into… making them.' How could he explain that every adult and teenager in Brocéliande had focussed every last drop of psychic energy on Y Tir the night of the raid in '32? And that time, they'd known it was coming. But now… They couldn't sustain that kind of focus indefinitely. E-Gov might strike at any time. 'The… detonators…' You have to find the right words not to faze them, he told himself. 'I'll talk to Gerhard,' he said quietly, feeling feeble, 'but they expire quickly. The Mutineers only have so much capacity to manufacture things that… powerful.'

'Thank you,' Dafydd said. 'We understand. And we want you to leave this room feeling like you've already made a big difference and we're grateful. Don't get the impression we're not, now.'

Again, there were nods and murmurs of assent around the room. It was so different from what he and Sian had been met with when they first arrived in Y Tir. Now, these people were his family, and he worried that one day soon he wouldn't be able to do enough for them.

Two days later, they made their way back from Anglesey to Y Tir in quiet shock. Emrys had driven in the van with Dafydd and Dewi. Gwen and Anwen had travelled with Tomas and Geraint in a farm truck. He could see the train of Y Tir vehicles behind them, mostly old electric vans and farm trucks using precious ethanol, and the one hydrogen bus they had liberated on a raid to South Wales a couple of years ago, all held together by the skill of Iolo and his son, Rhys. They used them as little as possible to preserve energy, but this had been a mass outing to bring back supplies for the whole community for the winter.

Instead, they were returning with nothing, the effort and energy wasted.

'I don't want you blaming yourself,' Dafydd said, breaking the tense silence.

'I don't understand.'

'I don't think there's much to understand, lad. They took your programmes and then took E-Gov's bribes as well and didn't deliver. It wasn't trade. It was betrayal.'

'If there's a hell they're well on their way to it,' Dewi added.

'They'll come for us now,' Emrys said, his voice almost a whisper.

Dafydd nodded. 'That's what I've been thinking. I know you said those detonators take a lot of… energy. But…'

'I'll leave for the forest tonight.'

Gerhard shook his head slowly. 'We can do it for a time. You know that, Emrys, but we don't know when E-Gov might attack. We can only keep up the cloaking here because we're so in tune with this land. The forest plays its own part. But…'

'I can do it.' Vivian stood in the doorway. 'Me and Morganne. We can do it together.'

Emrys and Gerhard stared at the slender twelve-year-old girl, dark-gold hair and quick blue eyes, the image of Lydie. Emrys expected that Gerhard would gently tell her how much she still had to learn but instead he said, 'Tell me more.'

Vivian smiled and came to the table to sit with them. 'I'm the lady of the lake, invisible to most outside the forest, able to hide in plain site. Who but another sorcerer can see the crystal palace beneath the lake or find the secret fountain of Barenton without me to guide them to it? I am Vivian and Eluned. I can become invisible and lead the lost through the otherworld, through Annwn.' She stared intently at Emrys. 'And your sister, Morganne, is as powerful as you, able to enchant and use illusion, able to stop people in their tracks or hold them in place.'

'But...' Gerhard began.

She held up a hand. 'Yes, all of us in Brocéliande can shift the perspective of those outside. In this magical place and with the help of the forest, we do it as we breathe. But me and Morganne, we can do it anywhere, more powerfully than anyone else. We just need to shift and...'

'For how long?'

'We're water spirits, Papa. If we have water, for as long as it takes. And I *am* ready.'

Gerhard sighed. 'You will need to travel back with Emrys?'

'Yes. I think the lake at Cwmorthin would be best.'

'I'll come with you. I...'

There was a knock and the cottage door was pushed open.

'I hear we're going on a quest,' Morganne said, stepping into the kitchen.

Myrddin Emrys

The runes change, but not the quest. There will be no ogham marked on bark skins, but maths and logic, software and magic. The tools change, but the quest is always for freedom.

What can I tell these good people whose existence is threatened? I will spin them a tale of resistance and protection and they will hear what they can.

And then we will go on doing what we always do, sorcerers and seers, shapeshifters and mystics—casting the runes, solving the maths, holding the light.

In the old stories Vivian was my apprentice, learning until she outstripped me, and that is as it should be. In this life she already has the power to change shape, and to shield those who are afraid for the fragile, precious community they have built.

In another life she was Gwenddydd, my sister, who took on the burden of prophecy when I could bear it no longer. In this life, Gwen carries that essence deep in the caves of her unconscious, yet her power is waxing and her healing will be strong.

And in yet another life Vivian was Eluned, who could blend with the forest, disappear from sight, and find her way in the Otherworld of Annwn. In this life the soul of Eluned has lived in Lydie and now lives on in Vivian and Anwen, their power growing day by the day.

And Morganne? Her courage and loyalty is the force of the tide. She will tolerate neither tyranny nor betrayal. She has been Artu's sister in other lives. In this life we shared a father, the man who has walked this earth as Rhydderch Heal and as Aurelius Ambrosius, the man who in each generation holds back the darkness for a time, a little time.

And this is what we will unite to do again. We will hold back the darkness until the light is reborn: myself, Myrddin Emrys, my sisters Morganne and Gwenddydd, my apprentice Vivian and my mentor Blaise. And Eluned, mysterious and powerful, coursing through Vivian and Anwen, overflowing with protection and healing.

Together, we will hold back the dark, for a little time.

15

The tension in the room was palpable. The members of the Gader had asked others to join them. Later, everyone from the villages would meet in one of the caverns below Cwmorthin, connected underground to Llechwedd, where once the caverns had been a home to them.

Gerhard looked around the room. 'I'm going to set up my base in the old cottage in Cwmorthin. Morganne and Vivian are already there.' He scanned the enquiring faces. 'Morganne is Emrys's half sister, Morfryn's child by one of our community, Ygraine. Sadly, no longer with us.'

He saw Anwen nod and Gwen startle.

'Gwenddydd is Merlin's sister, not Morganne,' he heard Gwen whisper to her mother.

He wanted to tell her that each time the story shifts slightly. No incarnation is ever the same as the last, but this was not the moment.

Dafydd finally voiced the question Emrys knew was in all their minds. 'We're grateful to you for coming, Gerhard. For bringing the detonators, but the girls… I just wonder if they'd have been safer…'

Gerhard smiled warmly. 'Don't let Morganne hear you calling her a girl.' He chuckled and went on, 'She's twenty-one and very much a young woman. My Vivian is only twelve, but the pair of them have done most of the work on the… cloaking detonators and I wanted them on hand. In any case, I don't know how long I'll need to be with you and we're approaching the first anniversary of losing Vivian's mother and baby sister. I couldn't leave her alone.'

'Oh, Gerhard, of course. I… We… We're so sorry…'

Gerhard shook his head. 'Nothing to apologise for. You're facing attack and I've turned up with two young women and a bag of buttons.'

A ripple of laughter punctured the tension.

'Okay, so tell us what we need to do.'

When the plan had been explained, in the language of technology rather than magic, Gerhard fielded questions. Finally he said, 'Of course, none of this solves the food shortages or the lack of other essential supplies. I need to get a fuller picture of what's most urgently needed and then I think the Mutineers will be able to help.'

'I can take you round the farms and supply barns tomorrow.' It was Tomas who spoke. 'We haven't had the best harvest, but it's not the worst either and we're always careful in how we use supplies. But the Mutineers are already doing so much for us and you have a community to feed too.'

'I'm not talking about anyone going without food. We've always had good trade with the underground organisation in Hungary and now they're in power and uniting the whole of Eastern Europe. They're good allies and, with the help of François and Emrys, we've expanded our trade with them. I think there may be a way to get supplies into the old harbour at Porth.'

Tomas let out a long sigh. 'I don't know how we could ever repay or thank you, but…'

'Just go on keeping Emrys safe,' Gerhard said. 'At least for another few years.'

Tomas shot him a quizzical look, eyebrows raised.

'I may need to borrow him for a couple of years eventually, but for now he's all yours… And I promise he'll always be back. But that's way ahead. For now, yes, let's do an inventory tomorrow. For today, let's all take some time to get ready for the assembly. That's more than enough for now.'

That evening, after the villages had come together and the buttons had been distributed, a small group met in the cottage opposite Cwmorthin lake. Gerhard had lit a fire in the big open grate and there was a pot of stew hanging above it, which he ladled into steaming bowls borrowed from Anwen.

Emrys looked at the ring that both Vivian and Anwen wore. In the dim light of the cottage each shimmered as though one moment it was not quite there and in another the ruby was flashing, from one hand to the other.

Vivian grinned at him. 'We are Luned,' she said simply.

Anwen nodded in agreement.

Gwen glanced around the room, looking from her mother to Morganne, from Vivian to Gerhard and Emrys. 'I feel so ordinary,' she said.

'You're Gwenddydd, sister of Merlin,' Morganne said. 'You're far from ordinary. Your father was Gwynne Rhydderch Hughes, an aspect of our king, like my father Morfryn Nazir Malik. You have his gift of prophecy and your mother's gift of healing.'

'She's right, Gwen,' Anwen added. 'Not everyone vanishes or shapeshifts, but everyone in this room has extraordinary gifts.'

Gwen studied Morganne. She had the same almond skin and aquiline features as Emrys, the same thick dark hair and deep brown eyes ringed in indigo.

'We're both his sisters,' Morganne said quietly. 'Me and Emrys look more alike, but that doesn't mean anything.'

'I just want to be able to help,' Gwen said wearily.

'You will,' Emrys reassured. 'People are going to need to stay in their houses. The only people going out will be for essential farming and we're going to limit that to very early mornings so that Morganne and Vivian only need to shield the whole area for short periods. It's easier to focus on the interior of buildings. That means anyone who is sick will have to be looked after at home. I've asked Gethin to co-ordinate the intrarnet. He'll pick up all the emergencies and I'll be focussing on making our communications impregnable to our friends across the border. You and Anwen will be the only ones from Y Tir able to move around at any time to help anyone who needs you. It could be for only a couple of days. But it could be months so there might be babies born, winter flu, deaths. It's a big job.'

'What about the others—Beddgelert, Llanberis and Ynys Mon?'

'The Mutineers have them covered. There are two shapeshifters in each community.'

'But how can I move around? I'm not like Mam. I can be seen,' Gwen pressed on.

'No, you won't be.' Vivian twisted the plaited gold band from her finger and handed it to Gwen. 'I won't need this while I'm a mermaid in the lake. Look after it and go well, Gwenddydd Rhydderch Hughes.'

Gwen gulped back tears as she slid the ring on. 'You know I'm still learning. I'm not…'

'You're a doctor as far as this community is concerned. You've been doing this since you were eleven,' Gerhard reassured, 'and taking it all in long before then.'

Gwen flushed and smiled, then said, 'Sorry to be full of questions, but what makes you think E-Gov might wait months?'

'Fear and hunger,' Gerhard answered. 'They know we didn't get the supplies. And they know that we will expect them to come for us. By leaving us longer, the community runs into shortages. People get frightened. They might figure some will even make a run for it.

They'll certainly think that stress and disharmony while rise the longer they make us sweat. They've been waiting to take down Y Tir for over twelve years. They'll want maximum pain.'

'It's so horrible,' Gwen said quietly, pulling a blanket closer around herself despite the fire blazing close by.

'But it's not going to happen,' Vivian said, moving towards Gwen to hug her.

Gwen smiled. 'No.'

'Absolutely not,' Morganne added defiantly. 'The supplies will arrive from Hungary. They'll go overland then by ship from Croatia, another good ally, and come into Porth.'

'And the harbour can take them?'

'Yes, we've got a work party to make sure any remnants of the old pontoons and moorings from the end of the '20s are lowered. As long as they come in on a high tide, they'll be fine. And it's good that the place hasn't been inhabited for so long.'

Gwen smiled again. 'I'm all questioned out and exhausted.'

Gerhard nodded. 'I think we all are. Let's say goodnight.'

Gwenddydd

And so we will do battle for the light, wielding our weapons of invisibility, illusion and healing. And I must save those I love so that one day my son and daughter will be born to become warriors of the light, as they do in each generation.

In this life, the house of Rhydderch Hael and the allies of Myrddin Emrys will not find themselves on opposite sides. My brother will not slay my children as he did long ago, its sad record in 'The Apple Trees' poem of *The Black Book of Carmarthen*:

> Now Gwenddydd loves me not and does not greet me
> —I am hated by Gwasawg, the supporter of Rhydderch—
> I have killed her son and her daughter.
> Death has taken everyone, why does it not call me?…
>
> Oh Jesus! would that my end had come
> Before I was guilty of the death of the son of Gwenddydd.

Yet my brother will know other sorrows in this life, griefs that might drive him mad if it were not for the hope of Artu, who he will bring into this world again.

First, we must survive this night, this long dark night.

16

Autumn slowly turned to winter. The supplies from Hungary arrived on ships from Croatia and Y Tir's barns and pantries were filled. The Gader met weekly in an online video space secured by Emrys and run by Gethin, their meetings increasingly lack-lustre as the weeks of house isolation and the tension of waiting mounted.

Anwen and Gwen found themselves making visits each day. Depression, stress and their physical analogues soared the longer people were confined. At the end of November, Iolo Bevan died of a hear attack. He and his son, Rhys, had kept the vehicles of Y Tir going for years and everyone wanted to be at the funeral but Gerhard insisted it must be a small gathering of family and a few representatives of the community, Dafydd and Tomas, Angharad and Anwen, who had asked Gerhard repeatedly whether she could have arrived at Iolo's cottage faster. But what could be swifter than the ring of Eluned? They all knew that nothing would have made the difference.

Samhain came, and with it the anniversary of the death of the Mutineers' leader, Morfryn Malik, also living as Gwynne Hughes. There were no community rituals but Morganne joined the Hughes' household for the evening and they told stories of the father that Emrys had never met and that Gwen could hardly remember and toasted others now dead. That night, Vivian held the shield alone, though Gerhard insisted on staying by the lakeside long into the night.

Solstice arrived with no communal rituals or Yule log burnt in the hearth of the Gader barn. No Lydie nor baby. Morganne insisted that this time she would hold the shield alone, as Vivian had at Samhain.

She glared at Gerhard when he suggested that at least he could be on hand to help her. 'I can do this,' her voice almost the hiss of cold water, Emrys thought, and full of determination. She and Vivian had spent most of each day in the lake since mid October and both looked well. 'Vivian did it for me when I was remembering my dad and you and Vivian need this space tonight. You need to do the ceremonies and remember Lydie and Innogen.'

Gerhard nodded. 'You're right about me and Vivian. But Emrys has also offered to help…'

'No. Emrys lived with you and Lydie for five years. I'm telling you, I can do this.'

And so Anwen, Gwen and Emrys joined Gerhard and Vivian in the cottage at Cwmorthin.

Gerhard filled glasses with red wine, adding water to Vivian's, as he had the previous year, and Vivian placed eight candles around the little table.

'There are candles for Maman and Innogen and one for Morganne, who is making this possible,' she said quietly.

When the lights were extinguished the darkness was total and Emrys could hear the crack in Gerhard's voice as he said, 'We come together for Alban Arthan. May the light of Artu be reborn in us as it is in Mabon, the Sun Child returning.'

'May the light of the constellation of the Great Bear lead us through the dark winter, back to Artu's light,' Vivian's voice was even shakier, and Emrys put out a hand to hold hers.

'May the Divine Child be born in each of us, to warm the earth and bring new life,' Gwen added, her voice almost a whisper.

'And may the Light of Winter, the Light of Artu, be with us as the seasons turn, and always,' Emrys finished.

It was Anwen who stood to strike the flame, lighting the remnant of last year's Yule log in order to kindle the new log, a gift from Tomas, moved early that morning while he was doing essential farm work. She lit a taper from the blazing oak and moved around the table, lighting the candles of those present and those absent.

'The light to you,'

'And also to you.'

When they were all seated again, Vivian stood and fetched a trail of mistletoe from a bundle by the fire, also brought by Tomas. She put a small piece in front of each of them, sat and grasped her glass with both shaking hands.

'May Druidh-lus bring you inspiration this year.'

They each raised a glass and sipped wine. Emrys took up the toast. 'May Druidh-lus bring you healing this year.'

Gwen sniffed back a tear. 'May Druidh-lus bring you guidance this year.'

And Anwen added, looking at Gerhard with so much compassion, Emrys wondered how it could be bearable, 'May Druidh-lus bring you fertility this year.'

They sat at the table for a long while, picking at the evening meal, thoughts wandering to those they had lost, to Morganne, holding the safety of all of Y Tir alone.

They hadn't the heart for stories or for sharing their fears and hopes for the coming year. After a while Vivian announced, 'I'm going to sleep in the lake.'

Gerhard startled and looked like he might argue, but then he nodded, stood and hugged his daughter. 'Your mother would be so proud of you.'

When Vivian had left to walk the few yards to the water, the sky stygian under the faintest sliver of crescent moon, they sat in silence until Emrys said, 'We should sleep. We never know what the next day will bring.'

'You're right,' Gerhard agreed, standing. 'Do you want to stay? Emrys could take the sofa and there's a tiny room that the girls used when we got here.'

'Thank you,' Anwen replied. 'But I for one think I'd like the walk, long as it is and the ring will keep us safe.'

Gwen and Emrys nodded agreement and they set off through the star-lit dark.

The raid came before dawn. The Regs came in more force than they had on the evening they'd left the caverns, smashing doors and leaving a trail of wrecked furniture and broken crockery as they clattered through what looked like deserted homes. A new tactic was to fire bullets as they rampaged through seemingly empty rooms.

They tore open sacks of grain and emptied metal bins of carefully stored vegetables and fruit, swearing at the stench of what they saw as rotten food.

Emrys sat in his room in the cottage in Rhyd, watching in shock, focussing hard alongside Morganne and Vivian, whose concentration was unwavering. He heard the Regs barrelling through the door and knew that Anwen and Gwen had already left to care for the wounded, moving invisibly with the ring of Eluned to protect them, though he knew it must be terrifying to be out amongst the spree of destruction.

The e-tablet buzzed in his hand. *Terrifying guys,* Gethin wrote. *They've shot holes in the walls in Nain's room, but she's okay. They're heading in here. They…*

'What? They what?' Emrys closed his eyes and took his vision to the Parry's house. Gethin was fine.

He looked shaken and his e-tablet was on the floor, cracked into two mangled pieces. So Gethin was out of the loop for alerting Anwen and Gwen to anyone who needed them.

Downstairs, the Regs moved out of the Hughes' cottage and Emrys let his vision move more widely across Y Tir. In Tanygrisiau, the Regs moved towards Ty Meirion. Emrys concentrated hard. Tomas and Geraint wouldn't panic, but he wished he could tell them to get into the tunnel behind the coal bunker where they'd have some protection from stray bullets. Would Geraint have his e-tablet with him? He tapped out a quick message. No indication that it had been read.

He concentrated on the house that seemed suddenly so far away as the Regs shattered its door, dry blue paint splintering as the wood cracked. Geraint wasn't in the kitchen.

'Pigging hole,' one of the Regs shouted. He fired a bullet into the glass lampshade above the big pine table. They made their way towards the bottom staircase, throwing open doors to the back bedroom, where Geraint had set up a study, clumped upwards in their heavy boots and into the large bedroom where Sion and Betsan had stayed during the last raid. Now it was Geraint's room, overlooking the vegetable plots and polytunnels that ran along the river.

They tipped up the bed and threw a desk across the room. Emrys watched Geraint shaking, the colour drained from him, huddling in a corner as a second Reg entered.

'You're right, absolute pigging hole. Must've been animals used to live here.' He raised his gun, pointing it at the far wall where Geraint crouched.

'No!'

His view of the room misted and went dark. He could hear Vivian, her voice watery, soothing as a summer stream, 'Shh, Emrys, shh. Breathe deeply. Fly! Fetch Gwen. Fly to Gwen.'

Emrys rushed to the door and threw it open, pausing on the threshold. Don't get yourself killed, he told himself. Breathe. Think. He held himself still for a moment, the calm flooding him, his bones becoming hollow and light as he soared, a falcon surveying the street, searching for Gwen.

Gwen looked up at the tapping on the window. A falcon? She pushed open the window and it was in and gone, replaced by...

'Emrys?'

'Geraint's been shot.'

He saw her flush then turn ashen, a tinge of green and she heaved.

'He's going to be okay, Gwen. I think he's... but he needs you.'

She wiped the stream of bile from her mouth on her sleeve.

'Are you finished here?'

She nodded. 'Stomach problems. Mainly stress and fear, I think. They're in bed now.'

'Go to Geraint.'

She was gone almost before the words were out. Was Geraint really going to be okay? He hadn't had time to look before Vivian told him to fly. But Tomas would be with him. He must leave Geraint to Tomas and Gwen. By now the Regs would be further down the village and Gethin couldn't get messages from anyone. He must keep track. He centred his breathing and… flew…

Epilogue

The group around Tomas's table looked haggard.

'Do you think they'll come again?'

Gerhard shook his head. 'No.'

'You sound certain.'

'The Standing Ground doesn't exist. I've just had confirmation from François. One of the things I asked him to set in motion was a protection treaty with the East European Confederation. A small team have been negotiating it since I arrived in Y Tir. It went through yesterday, to be signed today, which might explain their timing and their ferocity. Even if the Regs couldn't see you, E-Gov officials know you're here and they wanted to wreak maximum havoc before they honour their promise to back off and pretend you're an urban legend.'

'So how does it work?'

'Grain. E-Gov need it and EEC is the biggest provider. It's not the only commodity they need from them but it's top of the list of several essentials. EEC gets software from the Mutineers and from Emrys. You get 'forgotten' and E-Gov gets supplies. You'll also go on getting food and medicines from Hungary.'

Gwen came into the kitchen and the group turned to her as one.

Tomas stood up and hugged her. 'Thank you,' he said simply.

Gwen flushed and sat down. 'He's asleep. He was in a lot of pain but he's fine, thanks to Emrys alerting me.'

Anwen moved to fill the kettle, brushing a gentle hand across her daughter's head as she passed.

'And the girls?' Tomas asked.

Gerhard grinned. 'Girls?'

Tomas returned the smile. 'Young women. They're…?'

'Also asleep. Those two have slept and eaten in shifts mostly living in a lake…' He stopped. 'You must think we're strange creatures, Tomas.'

Tomas smiled. 'Best to keep quiet about things that aren't my business. I had my suspicions when it was only Gwynne who seemed… 'different'. But then Emrys arrived and I saw Anwen make Sian Hughes vanish that time Ifor Tigean's thugs were closing in on her… Not to mention listening to Anwen talk political strategy with this one when he wasn't even three…' He nodded towards Emrys, grinning. 'I don't ask questions about things that are beyond me, but I'm not daft.'

'Do you think there are others who think like you?'

'You know, I don't think they do for the most part. But perhaps that's the way they can handle things. Angharad and Gethin Parry probably have more than half an idea but I don't think anyone else knows or wants to know.'

'That's for the best,' Gerhard said. He glanced around the kitchen. Some clearing had already been done but signs of damage were everywhere. 'You've got a lot of mending to do.'

'We have,' Tomas agreed. 'But we've got food and promises of more to come. 2045 is a New Year. I just hope the peace lasts for a while.'

'Me too,' Gerhard agreed. 'And I think it will. Now, I'd better get some sleep myself. I think we'll be gone by tomorrow.'

He turned back as he reached the broken door of the house. 'The light to you,' he said, bowing slightly.

And they responded in unison, 'And also to you.'

Lightning Source UK Ltd.
Milton Keynes UK
UKHW041254130921
390503UK00007B/119